A Cowboy's Gentle Touch

SWEET VIEW RANCH
BOOK FIVE

JESSIE GUSSMAN

Contents

Acknowledgments

Cover art by Julia Gussman
Editing by Heather Hayden
Narration by Jay Dyess
Author Services by CE Author Assistant

Listen to the unabridged audio for FREE performed by Jay Dyess on the Say with Jay channel on YouTube. Get early access to all of Jay's recordings and listen to Jessie's books before they're available to the general public, plus get daily Bible readings by Jay and bonus scenes by becoming a Say with Jay channel member.

Chapter One

Lucas Clybourn took a deep breath as he put his hand on the library door and opened it.

He'd been in the library eight times since Christmas, and each time, he'd intended to ask the librarian, Ryland Solomon, out on a date.

Each time, he chickened out. Today, *today* was going to be the day that he actually did what he had been planning to do and ask the woman out.

It shouldn't be that hard. It's not like she was going to talk back to him or anything. After all, he wasn't sure he ever actually heard her say anything. At least not to him. Other than "may I see your library card please?"

Which, he had to admit, no one could say in a more sultry or romantic tone. It had given him goosebumps the whole way to his toes and back.

Cold North Dakota wind blustered down the street, and he hunched his shoulders as he pushed the door open.

The library opened three minutes ago. He'd been sitting in his truck for over fifteen minutes, waiting. He'd done the chores on the farm early, made sure the water was not frozen, and headed into town.

He didn't want there to be any other patrons in the library when he asked Ryland out. He had a feeling she might turn him down.

But the eight trips he made in the last two weeks surely counted for something. After all, that proves that they had something in common, right? Hefting the heavy armful of books he intended to return, he set them on the cart and walked further in, past her desk.

She stood at a display, her no-nonsense skirt falling below her knees. It was a librarian-colored navy blue, and the leggings she wore looked thick and heavy. As did her boots. They weren't heeled or stylish. They were flat and square, and they looked very warm.

She had a bulky sweater on. It was another library-dark color, and while it was not skin tight, it fell to her hips and emphasized the straightness of her slim figure. Her wavy hair, a dark brown color, fell to the middle of her back.

She moved slightly, and his eyes caught on her fingers, long and slender and very adept at arranging the books on shelves.

His heart started stuttering in his chest, and his feet slowed to almost a crawl, but she did not turn around.

Ryland Solomon was not exactly known for her effusive, bubbly personality.

That was him.

Except around her, he got all tongue-tied and couldn't seem to think of a single thing to say any time his eyes landed on her. It was like looking at her turned off the speaking part of his brain.

It also made his throat dry, and his tongue wanted to stick to the roof of his mouth.

Which was crazy, because he didn't have that reaction around anything. He was fearless, loved people, loved talking to anyone, loved being friends with everyone, and loved it when people loved him.

Maybe that's what made Ryland so interesting to him, because typically he didn't have a problem getting people to smile at him, talk to him, chat about anything with him. He could talk about literally anything.

Except with Ryland.

He didn't really think it was the challenge that drew him to her. Maybe it was the fact that she was so opposite from him.

He'd moseyed past her, and she hadn't lifted her head at all. It was like she knew it was him and didn't want to talk to him.

Normally he didn't have those kinds of thoughts. He didn't take anything personally and just assumed the best about people, automatically, without having to try to get himself to do it at all. It was just something he naturally did.

He sighed, walking to the first tall shelf and moving around it, paying no attention to the books on it, and trying to think about how he could find an excuse he could use to go back and say something to her.

She was a librarian. She could answer a question about a book.

Of course.

He grabbed a book from the shelf and walked back toward her, his steps slowing as he approached. She didn't lift her head to look at him at all.

"Is this a book you would recommend?" He held up the book he'd grabbed from a shelf.

She looked up at him and blinked. He didn't know how long she looked at him, but it felt like an eternity. Maybe a second or two. But still, that second or two dragged on and on and on.

Finally, she looked down at the book in his hand and tilted her head a little, maybe so it wasn't quite upside down and she could read the title better.

Without looking up, she began to speak. "*The Complete History of Public Farting. Everything you want to know about passing gas in public.*" She looked up, and there wasn't a smidge of humor on her face. "There are some books in this library that I have not read. That is one of them."

She waited maybe a breath longer, and then she turned back to her shelf.

So... Maybe it was the whole pride going before a fall. Or maybe it was just because he was a total idiot. But he had just thought he could talk to anyone about anything, but he had since found that there were subjects that he could not talk about with this serious and taciturn librarian. Public gas, its history and complete subject matter, was one of those things.

He could not think of a single thing to say.

He couldn't even get the words *thank you* out of his mouth.

Time ticked on, and he felt extraordinarily uncomfortable. Did he go back to the shelf and pick up another book to ask her about? Or did he decide he was going to check this book out anyway?

Every time he visited the library for the last eight times, he'd got at least eight books out. This would mess up his plan, and she might suspect that he was in here for something more than just picking up books.

"So, uh..." He cleared his throat. "Miss Solomon. Could you recommend a book for me?"

Man, he was such an idiot. If he was going to shove words out of his mouth, why didn't he say, *Miss Solomon, would you go out on a date with me?* Since that was the whole reason he was here.

She finished shelving the book in her hands and then picked up another book, holding it in both hands and twisting it a bit, slowly and carefully, as though she were thinking. "Typically when someone asks me to recommend a book to them, I ask what their interests are. However, since the last eight times that you have been here, you picked up books on rocks, the moon, alternate forms of psychology, competitive dog grooming, extreme ironing, and your fiction titles have included *The Great Gatsby*, the *Iliad*, *Middlemarch*, *My Best Friend is a Werewolf*, *The Man Who Could Not Kill Enough Fungus*, *The Secret Life of Jeffrey Dahmer*, and *Fifty Shades of Purple*."

He held up his hand. "That one was a mistake."

She raised her brows, and he immediately closed his mouth, feeling like the teacher had reprimanded him in front of thirty other students and slapped his fingers.

"Given that there has been such a wide range of titles from you in less than two weeks, books which you could not possibly have read before you returned them, I have to say that I couldn't and don't have a clue where your interest might or might not lie, and the only recommendation that I could potentially give you would be from the psychology section, and specifically, several books on bipolar disorder."

Right. So, he'd impressed her. He was pretty sure he'd impressed her.

"Would you like to go on a date?" So there, he got it out. So clunky and so unlike his typically suave deliveries. She was going to turn him down flat. He braced himself.

She looked back up at him, her brows high, her face a honeyed mask of absolute disdain. "The library is open late on Fridays and Saturdays. I would have to do it on Monday."

"I'll pick you up at six."

"My bedtime is at eight."

"I'll see you then." He thought maybe that was going to be the end of it, and he needed to hurry out so that he could do his fist pump and happy dance, without her noticing, then she added, "The psychology section is right over there."

"That's okay. I'll just take this one."

He held up the book in his hand and started walking toward the door.

"Just because I agreed to go on a date with you does not mean that you do not have to check that book out, sir."

"Oh. Yes, ma'am." He turned back around and stood at the desk.

She arranged two more books before she left her display and went to stand behind her desk. "You really ought to bring your library card, and then you can use the electric scanner in order to check out your books."

He almost said, *but then I wouldn't get to talk to you*, but he didn't. He didn't want to do anything that might jeopardize the fact that he had convinced her to go out with him.

Except, he hadn't really convinced her. She just said the absolute truth about him, because he was pretty sure he remembered most of those titles, not reading them, because he didn't actually read, but he did remember checking them out.

Honestly, he just went through random shelves in the library, pulling books and trying to catch glimpses of her over the top of or between the shelves.

Of course, there was the mess in the back of the library, shelves that needed to be put together, shelves that needed to be fixed, and a whole section of drywall that needed to be replaced because of the leak that happened last summer. He had avoided that section, even though it was the best area to get a glimpse of her since there were no shelves in the way.

He was so busy thinking about those things that she had his book checked out, handed it back to him, and walked away from her desk before he managed to think about getting his mouth moving.

He'd never met anyone that made him speechless. How did she do it? And as he watched her no-nonsense stride back to the display, he couldn't help but admire her. She...was so calm. Beyond his nervousness, beyond the fact that he couldn't get his mouth to work when she was around, there was a sense of peace that surrounded her, that drew him more than anything he'd ever noticed in a person before. How could she be so indifferent toward him? And how could he admire that so much?

Well, at least he had a date with her. Although, for the first time in his life he was going to have to practice speaking, because he didn't want to sit across the table from her and have absolutely nothing to say. He'd never done it before, but he could write a cheat sheet of things that he could talk about, in case his brain went blank as it had a tendency to do when she was around.

Yeah. That's what he'd do. There would be no long, awkward silences on this date. He was going to wow her and knock her socks off, and... He really didn't know where they would go from there.

Chapter Two

The entire date had been nothing but one long, awkward silence.

Ryland stared at the food on her plate. The silence was so long and so awkward, she hadn't even been able to eat through it. But she had rearranged her food completely. The peas, which had started out at the top left-hand corner of her plate, were now on the bottom right corner. The potatoes, including the gravy, had gone from seven o'clock to three o'clock, and the steak tips now sat directly at twelve o'clock, from their original position at five o'clock.

Her water glass was completely empty, and if she were able to speak, she would ask the waitress to fill it up when she came by, for the seventeenth time.

But neither one of them had been able to do more than nod or smile at the waitress every time she walked past.

At least Lucas had not been so debilitatingly awkward that he hadn't been able to eat. His entire plate was clean, and though he hadn't said a word to her, it was probably a good thing, because his mouth had been moving the entire time chewing his food.

"Are you going to eat that?" he asked, and she almost fell out of her chair.

He spoke. To her.

But he was pointing at her plate.

Now she had to talk. And she was not known as being glib or personable and definitely not a motormouth, all words that she'd heard used to describe Lucas. Charming, a people pleaser, and the biggest talker in Sweet Water were other common things she'd heard about him.

She wasn't sure exactly what he was talking about on her plate, but she didn't figure she needed to ask. She just put her fork down and pushed the entire plate across the table.

"Thanks." He grabbed her plate, shoved his empty plate over across the table at her, and dove into her rearranged food.

It didn't seem to bother him that it had been sitting in front of her for the last twenty minutes and was surely stone cold.

She sighed in her mind and wished, for the millionth time in her life, that she was a little bit different. That...she wasn't so debilitatingly shy and quiet that she couldn't seem to find her tongue, no matter how often she looked in the mirror and saw that it was right there in her mouth where it was supposed to be. Why couldn't she think of anything to say? And when she could think of something to say, like *waitress, may I please have another glass of water?*, why couldn't she say it?

The words just never seemed to come out of her mouth. Ever. Not small talk anyway. She could talk to people in the library who asked her questions. She could discuss books with people, and she could definitely talk to children. Children didn't make banal small talk about things that didn't matter to them. A child talked about things that mattered. A kid didn't talk about them unless they had something to say.

Adults, on the other hand, talked about stuff that...didn't matter. Like the weather. It was going to do what it was going to do, and it didn't matter what they said about it. It didn't matter if they complained about it, didn't matter if they knew what was going to happen, and didn't matter if they got twelve or fifty inches of snow.

She really didn't understand people's fascination with the weather, but that seemed to be what everyone talked about when they couldn't find anything else to discuss.

"It was a nice day out, wasn't it?" Lucas finally said something, after forty long, agonizing minutes of absolutely nothing, but it was the one topic that was almost guaranteed that she wouldn't be able to figure out anything else to say.

What was there to say about that? Just agree? She pretty much thought every day was a nice day. After all, weather came from the Lord, didn't it?

She looked down at the plate in front of her, the one he had scraped off and eaten every single molecule of food from.

If he'd licked it off, she'd missed it, but it kind of looked that way.

No. If he had licked it off, she would definitely have noticed. She had a hard time figuring out where to put her eyes. So she'd been doing a lot of staring at his plate, which was now hers.

It was mostly empty too. Seemed like when Lucas got nervous, he ate.

She was the opposite. When she got nervous, she didn't eat. Or talk. Or move.

It seemed like she and Lucas were opposites in a lot of things.

Maybe that's why she said yes when he asked her out on a date.

No, she'd had a crush on him for a long time, but he'd only recently started coming into the library. Eight times this year so far. And twenty or so times since last spring, when he first started coming in.

She definitely noticed him. How could she not? She didn't typically have tall, wide-shouldered, cowboy-boot-wearing, charming men walk into the library.

Of course, he wasn't charming with her. At first, she thought he hated her, since he never said anything to her, other than *can I check this book out, please?*

Which, she had to admit, he had the nicest voice she'd ever heard. It was...swoon worthy. Definitely romance novel worthy.

But other than that, she only ever got to hear him speak when he was talking to someone else. Not her.

Well, she knew what she would never want to do again, and that was go on a date with him. And he would never want to go on a date with her, either. After all, they barely said five words to each other the entire evening. Talk about a major disaster.

He paid the bill, and she was grateful to realize that at least he hadn't flirted with the waitress. As charming as Lucas could be, after not saying a word to her all evening, he could have charmed the socks off the waitress. But he hadn't. That was a point in his favor anyway.

It wasn't like she thought he didn't have character. Everyone in town said he did; the Clybourns were a well-respected family, and not just because of their name, which really didn't mean anything in Sweet Water, since they were new. It was because of the way they conducted business, the way they treated people, and their general conduct around town. They were good, honest, hardworking people who could be counted on to do the right thing.

Even if Lucas was quite chatty and charming. Except when he was with her.

He did open her car door as the wind buffeted them and the forecasted snow blew down.

They didn't often get the kind, sweet, happy snow that happened in romantic movies. Not in North Dakota. Snow in North Dakota came down with a purpose. Often, it came down sideways. But regardless of the way it came down, it did come down, and quite often, it came down most of the winter.

That was why she barely went anywhere in the winter, other than to get groceries.

Lucas stopped at the library, and as she gathered up her purse and tugged on her hat, he jumped out, hurrying around and opening her door.

He offered her his hand, and looking at the piles of plowed snow beside the pickup between her and the sidewalk, she didn't have to think about whether or not she wanted to take it. She wore what she always did, serviceable clothing that would keep her warm, including boots with plenty of traction, but that plowed snow could be icy and dangerous, and she put her hand in his.

Even through their gloves, it felt...different. Odd. But somehow perfectly right.

She wanted to roll her eyes. If the date was a disaster, just because he had nice hands didn't mean that she would go out with him again, not that he was going to ask.

He walked beside her, in the same silence they had spent the rest of the evening, to her door, where she got the key out and handed it to him. He seemed to be waiting for it. And he took it, unlocking her door.

He handed it back to her, but as she took it, he held onto it for just a second. "Next Monday, same time?"

"Yes."

He let go of the key, and she walked into her home and closed the door behind her.

She just agreed to another date?

That was crazy. And...he asked her out on another date? Why? He couldn't possibly have had a good time. They didn't say *anything* to each other.

Shaking her head, although she wasn't sure whether she shook it at herself or at him, she turned the light on, moved into her small apartment, and started taking her winter things off. This called for a cup of hot chocolate and a good book, possibly one that would last the entire night.

Chapter Three

"I don't understand how this water line froze. We had heat tape on it."

Lucas was just talking to hear himself talk. And Tobias just grunted. Which was what Tobias did. Grunted, and he was really good at silences too.

Which maybe was why Lucas and he got along so well. Lucas didn't shut up, and Tobias didn't talk. So they got along really well. Except, now Lucas wanted to know why Tobias never talked. So, when the water line had frozen, and they needed to go out to the barn and follow it, and then switch out the broken ends, he figured it was a good thing for him to help with.

On the Clybourn dude ranch, he had been the one to do most of the guest activity last summer. He was the outgoing, personable one who always got along with everyone and was a natural choice to be the leader of all the groups that went out and the coordinator for the activities around the ranch.

Last summer had been their first summer, and he thought it had gone really well. They had great reviews online and bookings for this spring, summer, and fall. But since he'd done the majority of the work over the summer, and because there weren't too many guests who wanted to stay in North Dakota in January, he had a light load.

Maybe that was why he spent so much time in the library. He'd had his eye on Ryland since last spring, but because he was so busy, he couldn't ask her out. Although, when he finally got around to asking her, and she said she wanted to go on Monday nights, he realized that he probably could have done it. Typically on the dude ranch, the groups went out on Friday nights and Saturdays, sometime Sunday nights, but Monday was often his day off.

Figures.

If he could get his mouth open when he was around her, it would help things a lot.

Tobias held a torch, something that they had to be careful with, because if they held it in one spot for too long, it would melt the plastic the pipe was made of. But it was the best thing to thaw the lines out, so they both had a handheld propane torch that they used, moving them constantly.

He kept his gloves on, because they were in the middle of a huge deep freeze, and the temperature outside was minus twenty. That was not including the windchill. Which made it even worse.

He hoped the library heat did not go on the fritz.

Across the country, there were a lot of schools closed, but not in North Dakota. Here, things were liable to get colder before they got warmer.

"How'd your date with Ryland go?" Tobias asked, which made Lucas snort.

It had been last night, and it had gone terribly. But what did he say?

"Would you believe that I couldn't get a word out of my mouth the entire time?"

"You?" Tobias looked up at him and almost forgot his torch. It would cause a lot more work if they melted a hole in the pipe. It would involve shutting off the water, switching out the pipes, and he definitely did not want to do that, especially in this cold.

"Pay attention," Lucas said.

"Don't say such unbelievable things."

"I know. The crazy thing is, it's true. I couldn't get a word out of my mouth to save my life."

"When has that ever happened?"

"I don't know. And actually, that's not entirely true. I did manage to point to her plate and say 'are you going to eat that?'"

"Tell me you didn't eat her food."

"I did. You know how I am when I'm nervous. Everything that's within reach of my mouth goes in it. Even if it's not entirely edible."

"Yeah, I remember that one time when you were nine you ate toilet paper. It was...awkward when the school counselor recommended you have a psychological evaluation."

"Yeah. I think that was what convinced Mom to start homeschooling."

"It was either that or they were going to put you in a straitjacket."

"It wasn't that bad."

"You have a knack for being able to look on the bright side. Good for you."

"Well, there's really no way to look on the bright side of our date, except...when I dropped her off at her apartment, I figured that was probably the worst evening she'd ever had, that I was the worst date she'd ever had—"

"Excuse me, but I doubt that Ryland has dated that much."

"Yeah. You're probably right. I haven't, either. That's probably one of the reasons she's so intriguing to me. She... It's like we have so much in common, even though we're total opposites. Does that make sense?"

"I guess. If you say it does," Tobias said as he shut off his torch and tapped on the lines to see if they could hear the ice.

"Still frozen solid," Tobias said, then lit his torch up, and started holding it on the line again.

"So what made it so it wasn't a complete disaster?" Tobias asked, after they started working on the line again.

"Well, I stood at the door, after I opened it for her and held the key out for her. She took it from me, and I don't know. I mean, I love her hands. It wasn't anything that I saw, it was just that I didn't want to let her go. So I said, 'Next week, same time?'"

"And she said, 'Not on your life.'"

"No. She said yes."

"No way."

"Yeah. So I let go of the key, she walked into her apartment and closed the door, and that was it."

"So you bought her dinner, you ate it, and then you dropped her off, without saying anything to her all evening, and she agreed to go out with you again?"

"Yes. I'm not sure why she agreed to go out with me in the first place. She totally called me on everything that I've done. Made fun of all the ridiculous books that I've borrowed from the library. Did you know someone actually wrote a book on extreme ironing?"

"And you checked it out of the library?"

"I need to start watching what I do. You know I haven't read a book in my life before, other than what Mom made us do to finish school. I mean, it's a lot more fun to talk to people than it is to read about people."

"All right."

"Anyway, I just didn't pay attention. When I'm in the library, it's like all I can do is try to get my eyes on her. It's...weird."

"Yeah. Maybe you should stop trying to go out with her."

"I can't. It's like I'm obsessed. Do you think she, I don't know, cast a spell on me or something?"

"Are you sure you've not been influenced by the odd books you've been checking out?"

"Yeah. I'm sure. It's... It's just so strange."

"Sorry. But I'm not sure I can help either one of you. You both seem to be a little off."

"I see where I'm odd. But you think Ryland is odd, too?"

"I guess. She agreed to go out with you to begin with, and then after having a miserable time, she agreed to go out with you again."

"That's just it. If you were on a date, you probably wouldn't say much of anything either."

Tobias lifted his shoulder underneath the sheepskin jacket he wore. "I guess it depends."

"You typically don't talk much." Lucas closed his mouth. He didn't want to offend his brother, although Tobias wasn't exactly known as having a hair-trigger temper or anything. He was one of the more patient of his siblings. "What makes you talk?"

"I don't know. I guess when I feel comfortable. Sometimes I don't feel comfortable. Plus, I can't do two things at once, you know, feel uncomfortable and talk at the same time."

"You think that that's what her problem is?"

"You're not exactly known for making people uncomfortable. In fact, of all the people I know, you probably are the best at putting people at ease. You make them laugh, you make them smile, and you have them talked into whatever it is you wanted them to do before they even realized you were talking them into anything."

"Wow. A compliment. I think?"

"I don't know. Maybe it was."

"But I wasn't charming her. I guess... I guess all that stuff I do with everyone else is a discussion of surface stuff, you know? I want to be deeper with her. But I don't really know how. I'm so used to just doing all the surface-level, insincere, easy compliments that are mostly true but I don't have a lot of feeling or sincerity behind, and she...she just makes me feel deeper. And that's the other thing, when I'm around her, even though I'm crazy nervous around her, she just makes me feel calm. Like I've stepped into a pool of clear, calm water that is just laughing and relaxing and... I don't even know. But just being around her seems to help me focus my thoughts, even if I can't open my mouth."

"Well, I don't think that will last forever. You'll be able to talk to her eventually."

"I've been going to the library since April. It's been almost nine months, and I haven't even gotten a 'nice hair' out of my mouth. Or—"

"You asked her out."

"It was the most awkward way I've ever asked anybody anything. I mean, I probably asked two or three women out on dates. But never like that."

Their family hadn't been big on dating. Their parents had always told them that if they were interested in someone, the best way to get to know them was to work with them. That was what would show them a person's character, how hard and long and well they work. They always encouraged them to invite potential love interests over and spend time with their family. Anyone who could handle twelve siblings all at once could handle pretty much anything. And if they couldn't handle the family, the parents said that maybe they weren't right for them.

They'd had plenty of people over, but their parents had died more than a decade ago in a car accident, and while Lucas tried to do what he'd been raised to do, dating was just easier. After all, he could hardly imagine inviting Ryland over to the farm. He'd never actually seen her out of the library, although he assumed that she probably went to the grocery store at least. Got gas, went to appointments.

Although, maybe she didn't. Maybe she was a total recluse, and he didn't even know it. Although, she got those librarian clothes from somewhere. Maybe there was a special library clothing store online, where a person could order clothes that made them look like a librarian.

He actually kinda liked those. The long skirt she wore was modest and serviceable, and she seemed like a no-nonsense kind of person, although...he'd seen her laughing and joking with kids, and that had made him want to try to get her to do it with him. Except...he had this small problem about not being able to talk to her.

"If someone were trying to get you to talk, what would work?" he asked Tobias as they shut their torches off and checked the water. It ran.

Lucas breathed a sigh of relief. It was cold out, and he was ready to go back inside and get warm. And get food. He was definitely hungry.

"I don't know. I guess I'd talk about something that's interesting to me. Which is typically not stuff that's interesting to anyone else. But also, I don't want to feel like I'm being judged for my words. Sometimes it takes me a while to think about the right ones, and sometimes people don't give me enough time to get the words out."

He looked over his shoulder, then turned the water off, grabbing the hose that lay on the floor and hooking it back up.

"If you use this, don't forget to drain it."

"All right."

Lucas looked at the tape that held the hose together, more tape than hose, it seemed, and that triggered something in his brain.

"Have you heard anything about our financial situation lately?" he asked.

They had all agreed that they weren't going to talk about it over

Christmas. They didn't want to ruin the holiday season by trying to figure out how they were to keep the ranch afloat for one more year. Everything seemed to be taking off, but it was really difficult to start a business and have it be profitable immediately. Usually it took a little bit of time and an awful lot of work to get things going. They'd all been working as hard as they could, and they could see the light at the end of the tunnel, but before Thanksgiving, Ezra, their oldest brother, had said that it was going to be real tight to get through the winter. Especially if they had to buy hay.

"I think Ezra was going to call a meeting about it in a few weeks if things didn't turn around. Which, nothing's going to turn around at this point. Not until spring." Tobias didn't sound upset, but it definitely wasn't happy news.

"So what's the meeting going to be about?"

"I guess we wouldn't need a meeting if we all knew."

"Is he going to say that we need to find work off the ranch?"

"Maybe. Or we're going to need to figure something out."

"How bad is it?"

"I think he said something about it was going to take close to six figures, and even then, he didn't know whether it would be enough."

"Wow."

That dampened his enthusiasm. It wasn't a matter of him not knowing what he would do if they had to sell the ranch. All of his siblings were resourceful and industrious. They would all find something, but the ranch had been a dream of their parents, and each one of them had caught the vision. All twelve of them had plans to make the ranch their permanent home. And their permanent job. They all pitched in, even though a couple of their youngest siblings were still in college.

"I think the reason that he's holding the meeting off until February is because he doesn't want anyone to sit around and worry about it. So don't. But if you can find something to do that will be a help, or you think of something, don't hesitate to say."

He couldn't think of anything that would bring in six figures in a matter of months. Unless he robbed a bank. And he wasn't interested in doing that. Although, he supposed in prison he'd have plenty of people to talk to.

But charming a judge was much different than trying to charm guests on the ranch. And he really loved the great outdoors. He wasn't sure whether he could handle being cooped up for years.

He didn't know what the going sentencing length was for bank robbers. And he wasn't interested in finding out.

They put their tools away and walked to the barn door.

"You know, sometimes God just makes things obvious to us. Sometimes it takes us a little while to open our eyes. Ryland seems like a nice girl, and maybe she's the right girl for you. Maybe God just wants you to learn to be...still for a little bit. And maybe Ryland's who He's going to use to teach you that."

"Are you trying to tell me that it's not always necessary to talk?"

"Maybe. Maybe I'm just saying, be open to what God's trying to get you to do. Don't think that you know."

They walked through the barn door, kicking the bottom of it so that it unfroze from the ground before they opened it.

He wasn't sure exactly what Tobias was saying, but often Tobias had hidden wisdom in his words. Something that Lucas never really had. He just spit out words without thinking and oftentimes regretted it. Maybe that's what God wanted him to learn. That in the silence, he didn't have to be panicking about what he was going to say; rather, he could be weighing his words. And speaking more carefully.

An interesting thought.

Chapter Four

"Oh my goodness. Come on in!" Ryland said as she opened her door to see Ellen Feagley and Rosie Stryker standing on the other side.

The library didn't open until noon on Wednesdays, and Ryland was having a late brunch. She had stayed up all night the night before reading a romantic comedy that had been set in Good Grief, Idaho.

She'd thought that was such an odd name and figured that the author had made it up for the series, but when she went to look it up, she realized that there actually was a town named Good Grief.

It wasn't the same town, but...it might be a town that she'd want to visit sometime.

Anyway, she ended up reading the entire book, which was the third or fourth in the series, and got a kick out of the author making fun of herself.

She was a little embarrassed about the underwear scene, but she actually knew the narrator who had been mentioned in the book, and she agreed that he was very dreamy.

He was also probably very warm, since he did not live in North Dakota.

The ladies walked in, stomping their boots off by the door before peeling off their hats and gloves.

"I brought this for you," Rosie said as she held up a book entitled *The Cowboy's Marriage Mistake*. "I saw it in the discount bargain bin. They were giving the last of the books away for free. Apparently they couldn't even give this one away, but there was something about it that was compelling, so I took it home and read it, and it could almost be Cord's and my story word for word. Uncanny similarities." She shook her head and waved the book around. "I just had to bring it and see if you had a spot for it on your shelf?"

"Of course," Ryland said, taking the book from Rosie. She certainly wouldn't say no to Rosie, who had been the original librarian in Sweet Water. She had fought to keep the library open, worked in it without pay, and then spearheaded the effort to raise money to build a new one after the first one had burned down.

They had built the second one very similar to the first, with an apartment for the librarian attached. It was perfect for Ryland, who never planned to get married and figured she would never have children. She had always been somewhat socially inept, and the idea of actually having a husband, while it was a nice thought, she would have had to talk to someone in order to get them to ask her to marry them, at least she assumed that was the way it worked, and so far, that hadn't happened.

Thankfully, her inheritance made it possible for her to live on her librarian's salary, and she was content. She could read as much as she wanted to, order in the books she wanted to read, and she got to talk books on an almost daily basis.

Because of her job, she'd developed a friendship with Rosie, whom she loved. Rosie often stopped in when she was in town, and Ryland had a deep respect for her. Not only had she raised their children, but she helped her husband on the farm too. Still did. Now that most of her kids were out of the house, Ryland wouldn't be surprised if she wanted the library job back. But she also seemed happy on the farm.

"I hope you have some good news for us," Ryland said to Ellen. The last time Ellen had been in, they had talked about how Ellen was hoping to have a baby and was excited about starting a family with Travis.

But her face dropped.

"No. No baby so far. I actually said something to Travis about going to the doctor to find out if there was a problem, but...he didn't exactly laugh, because he knows it's important to me, but he did say that maybe we ought to give it a year or two of trying." Her cheeks pinkened a little. "He said he enjoys trying." She smiled a little. "I do too."

Ryland could feel her own cheeks heating. But Rosie didn't seem the slightest bit bothered.

"If God gives you a few years without any children, enjoy them. The trying gets a little bit more difficult as the children arrive, and you get swamped with all the busyness that they entail. Not that I don't love my children, but...it's much nicer now that they're older, and we have the house to ourselves sometimes. It's...kind of like when we were first married." She grinned, and Ryland could only imagine what in the world was going on at their house. She made a mental note not to pop in unexpectedly.

It made her a little sad though, that the two ladies were smiling about the fun they had with their husbands, and she felt left out.

"I heard that you had a date," Rosie said, looking at her with her brows lifted like she was hoping Ryland would give her the details.

"Well, I was myself on the date. I didn't say anything. Like, not five words. So, I have solidified my reputation as the most boring date in the universe."

"You don't have to talk to be interesting," Ellen said, and her cheeks hadn't quite gone back to their normal color.

"I didn't do anything to be interesting at all, just sat and stared at his plate of food while he ate it, and then sat and stared at my plate of food while he ate that too."

"You mean he took you out for dinner and he ate your food?" Rosie said before she broke into laughter as Ryland nodded.

"I don't think that you have solidified your reputation as the worst date anywhere. I think that might be him," Ellen said with a chuckle.

"Well, he might as well have eaten it, because I wasn't going to. I can't eat when I'm nervous, and going out with Lucas definitely made me nervous."

"You know, all joking aside, I kinda think that you and Lucas would be perfect for each other. He never shuts up, and you never talk, and that should make for a really great couple."

"He didn't talk either," Ryland said, and she still hadn't figured that out. It seemed so out of character for him.

"Oh my goodness. That means he really likes you!" Ellen said, sounding thrilled about the prospect.

"I don't know. He really didn't act like he did." Ryland wasn't making that up. He...didn't seem like he enjoyed her company at all.

"Yeah. I don't know. If he wasn't able to talk to you, maybe you made him uncomfortable. I mean, if Lucas wasn't saying anything, that's very unusual."

Ryland nodded, because she agreed more with Rosie than with Ellen. The fact that Lucas couldn't find anything to talk to her about just said that they weren't as compatible as she'd like for them to be.

"That's too bad. Maybe he would have loosened up if you guys would have managed to get along well enough to have a second date."

"That's the thing. When he was standing at my door, just before I went in, he said 'same time next week?' And...after I had just thought that I was never going to go out on a date with him again because it was the worst date in the history of the world, I said yes, then I walked inside and he left."

"Wow. That..."

"...sounds like something from a horror movie," Ellen said, finishing Rosie's sentence.

The three of them laughed together.

"Right? Why can't I be normal?" Ryland said, in a bit of a dramatic flair that was not her usual. Typically she was pretty stoic and didn't have too much trouble taking things as they came rather than bemoaning about things she couldn't change. But she put her head down on the table, feeling like there was something majorly wrong with her. Why did she have to be so weird?

"You are normal. There are tons of people like you. Who do you think runs these libraries all across the nation?" Rosie said, rubbing her shoulder a little. "Also, I used to be the exact same way. My twin was outgoing and vivacious, and I was serious and quiet."

"How did you ever get married? You couldn't have been as bad as me."

"I think I was worse in some ways. But...Cord was my friend. I'm not even sure how, maybe because we went to school together, and my twin broke the ice first, but we were just always really good friends."

"That's the way Travis and I were, although I didn't typically have a problem talking to people. So I don't relate as much."

"But you guys managed to find guys to be friends with, and then you built something more on that. I can't even be friends with anyone, because I can't get enough words out of my mouth when I'm around a man. Any man."

"Men can be intimidating. They're big and often loud and sometimes obnoxious. Even the good ones."

"Or they're charming, except when they're around me, and then they're...not. Because I seem to bring out the worst in everyone."

Now she knew she was just being doom and gloom, and she tried to push those things aside. She didn't want to be the negative Nelly that brought everyone's mood down. So she lifted her head and gave a tremulous smile. "But I'm actually really happy here. I mean, being a librarian is my dream job. I get to read as much as I want to, I have a really cozy and nice apartment, and my job isn't too demanding. I have plenty of time to be outside, especially in the summer."

"That's a good way of looking on the bright side. But I wouldn't write yourself off. I used to be shy and retiring, very much like you in fact... I recall hiring someone to give me kissing lessons."

"You what?" Ryland couldn't believe it, and Ellen looked shocked as well.

Rosie nodded her head. "I kind of forgot about that, but actually I think it was my twin who hired him. But I needed it. I had no idea how to kiss anyone, and I really wanted to get Cord's attention. Someone told me that kissing does that to a guy. Good kissing."

"How did it go? Were the lessons...beneficial?" Ryland considered the idea. Could she hire someone to teach her how to kiss? She certainly had no idea. Nothing except what she read in books, and that seemed to be more imagery—the world shook, and it tilted on its axis, and her heart beat faster and her breathing was hard, and...they didn't really go into the mechanics of where to put your teeth, so they didn't get in the way, and what exactly she was supposed to do with her mouth during the kissing. And goodness, she could hardly even think about her tongue and where it would go. It seemed like an awful lot to keep track of, especially for someone like her who had a tendency to be clumsy. Could she work her lips and tongue and teeth while still standing and... what would she do with her hands?

"Actually, I decided that I wasn't going to take lessons from him. It's a long story, but...someday maybe I'll write a book about it." She looked at the book Ryland had set on the table. "This book is very similar to my story. If you read that, you'd get the gist of it."

"Are there kissing lessons in it?"

"Yeah. There are." Rosie had a bit of a faraway look in her eye, like she was remembering those years from long ago, and they were good memories. "But no. I ended up only kissing Cord. It...seems to be something that happened naturally, and I don't think I really needed the kissing lessons. But I suppose they might be beneficial for someone. Just not me. Plus, I didn't really want to kiss anyone except Cord."

Well, that could be a problem. She hadn't really considered that. If someone were going to give her kissing lessons, she had to kiss them, and...she really didn't want to kiss anyone. Except for Lucas. She could totally imagine herself kissing Lucas. But even though she had a good imagination, it was hard to picture herself kissing anyone else.

"I didn't kiss anyone except Travis, and I think we kind of learned together. That makes it fun. I mean, if you're with someone who thinks skillful kissing is a good thing and wants you to be a skilled kisser before you get together, then that might be an issue, but Travis and I were both pretty willing to learn on each other. It made things a little awkward on our wedding night, but we have some really fun memories."

Ryland thought that was probably the best way. It seemed like it was definitely the Christian way, and it was a good way to look at it too. She'd heard a lot of people say that they preferred to have someone who knew what they were doing, but...wasn't that the point of getting to know each other? Wasn't that the fun of being married?

Of course, she, with her no experience at all and inability to even get any experience, probably wasn't the person to be thinking about it.

After all, what did she know? Only what she'd read, and the experience of one terrible, awful date that somehow garnered her an invitation for another date, although she wasn't even sure why.

"You think he just asked me out on another date because he didn't want to hurt my feelings?"

"That's a distinct possibility. Lucas is very concerned about hurting people's feelings. He's so people focused, and I think that's part of what makes him so charming. He wants to make sure everyone around him is happy."

"I'm not sure I want to be with someone who's concerned that everyone else is happy. Is that terrible?" Ryland put the question out there, even though she thought that maybe it made her seem like a bad person.

"I don't think that's terrible at all. You don't want to be married to someone who is always looking at other people and trying to make them feel good about themselves. Or trying to impress them, or have them give him positive attention."

"No. You want your husband to be focused on you. I mean, you don't want him to be a jerk to everyone else, but you don't want him to look at whoever's in front of him, or the newest person in his life, and see him trying to impress them. That would be...terrible." Ellen shivered with revulsion.

That is exactly what Ryland thought. She didn't know Lucas well enough to know if that's the way he'd be, but since he was everyone's friend, she could see that being a distinct possibility.

"I'm the exact opposite. I mean, I think I'm nice to people, but the only people I'm really super concerned about are the people who are in my deepest inner circle. You know?"

"Yeah. That's the way introverts often are. Exceptionally loyal, and very considerate of their friends, they make the best kind of friends, but they only have a few."

"Partly because you can't give that kind of loyalty and attention to the entire world. You have to narrow it down to a select few."

They sat for just a moment, like everyone was thinking about what they'd been talking about, then Rosie said, "This is a total subject change, but I wanted to ask if you would be okay delivering a meal to

Agathe. The ladies in town have all been trying to make sure that we give her at least one or two meals a week. She's...struggling."

"How has her husband been doing?" Ryland asked, concerned. Agathe had spent a lot of time in the library since Ryland had taken over as librarian, and she loved the lady. She was so sweet and had such fun tales of growing up in the countryside of France, so different than North Dakota.

"He's slowly getting worse. That's the diagnosis, and it doesn't surprise anyone, but I think this part has been the hardest on Agathe, because she really has to face the fact that this is the way it's going to be. It's never going to get better. And it doesn't really matter what kind of positive spin you try to put on it, nothing changes."

Ryland swallowed and nodded. That would be so hard. She couldn't imagine how difficult it must be to watch someone she loved, had spent a lifetime with and built a beautiful life with, slipping away day by day.

It almost seemed like it would be easier to lose him all at once.

"Of course. I would love to take her something. Do you have a specific date?"

"We usually try to aim for Tuesdays and Fridays so she's not getting a meal two days in a row. We don't have anything scheduled, so pick what day you want and just let me know. I think she just appreciates us supporting her. I...don't know how else to show we care and to help her."

"Yeah. That's tough."

"We do have people staying with him on Saturdays so she can go to her support group meeting. If you'd like to volunteer for one of those days, or if you'd like to take your meal that day and just go ahead and stay, that would be fine too."

"Maybe I'll message her and see what she says," Ryland said, knowing that messaging someone was a lot easier for her than calling them on the phone. There was just something about talking to someone, whether it was in person or over the telephone, that was hard, but messaging wasn't quite as difficult. And this would be for a good cause. She could do it.

It wasn't long after that that Rosie and Ellen left, and Ryland fingered the book that still lay on the table. Maybe someday she'd have her own story. She hoped so. And while she saw that kissing lessons probably weren't the smartest thing in the world, it was really tempting to look into it. After all, kissing didn't involve talking, and she already knew she was terrible at talking. Maybe she would be better at kissing.

Chapter Five

This date hadn't been any better than the last three.

Lucas sat in the steakhouse in Rockerton, wishing that he could figure out what in the world his problem was.

He'd been able to get a couple of lines out of his mouth, but they had been banal and trite. Something about the weather, which, it was North Dakota in February, and the weather was cold and snowy. Big surprise there. People had been talking about the cold, snowy weather for months, and there really wasn't anything more to say about it, other than how long did they think it was going to last? And he might have actually posed that question to Ryland, but it made him feel like an idiot when she looked at him and shrugged her shoulders. Obviously, she didn't know any more than what he did.

She did manage to get a word or two out, which...was pretty much what she did on each of their dates. Three times, they had a date, and at the very end of each evening, he somehow managed to get the words out to ask her on another one, and she somehow managed to say yes each time.

How long was she going to put up with sitting in front of him staring at him and neither one of them saying anything for the entire evening before they gave up and admitted that this just wasn't working?

Maybe he should start a conversation about how their dates weren't working and they should not date anymore. But he probably would still end up asking her out on another date at the end of the evening. Those words seemed to come out of his mouth unbidden.

He pushed around the last of her steak. That was another thing. Every time she ordered food, and every time he ended up eating it for her. Every time, he told himself the next time he wasn't going to eat her food, but...then the next date came, and she didn't eat it, and it sat over there on her plate looking delicious and very lonely, and...before he knew it, he was asking if he could have it.

Except for today, all he'd done was finish his plate and push it a little bit aside, and without saying anything, she pushed her plate over to him. He looked at her, she lifted her shoulder, and then he grabbed her plate, slid it in front of him, and dug in.

The steak was cooked perfectly. Still red in the middle and seasoned just right. It was delicious. One of the best steaks he'd ever eaten.

He supposed that made this a good date.

Problem was, it was going to be their last.

He'd been thinking about what he could do to save the farm, and he'd hit upon a solution, but...it would mean no more dates with Ryland. Which had honestly been the hardest part of him making the decision.

The waitress came back, asking if she could fill up their glasses, and rather than answering, Ryland simply handed her her water glass.

The waitress smiled and walked on. She'd already filled his glass up twice, and all he'd done was point to it.

She mentioned what she thought he had to drink, and he nodded, and she brought back a fresh glass.

He had to admit, he didn't feel any pressure to be someone he wasn't when he was with Ryland. She seemed content with his silences, and other than castigating himself for not being a very entertaining date, he actually felt...free. He didn't have to talk if he didn't want to, and so far, anyway, she'd always agreed to go out with him again. He almost was at the point where he wanted to try to see if he could get her to go out with him, even though he *never* talked to her.

Except, this was it. The end. Their last date. Ever.

As he finished her plate, she began to fidget. That was so odd that it caught his attention. Normally she sat calmly, quietly, of course, and with patience. Like she could sit still all day and stare at him eating.

But today, she started moving, folding up her napkin, then unfolding it again. Normally she didn't play with the stuff around her. Just quietly kept her hands...he didn't even know where. In her lap maybe.

He wanted to ask about it, but talking just seemed...odd after they hadn't said anything all evening, and he wasn't sure what he was going to say anyway. "Why are you moving?" Like she wasn't allowed to or something? That seemed silly.

It was sad though, because he wanted to know so much more about her. What she was thinking, what she liked, what she wanted, but maybe it was a good thing that he didn't know. He might end up liking her more than he already did, which was pretty much as much as a person could like a person they'd never talked to. Just spending time in her company made him feel...relaxed.

He wasn't asking her for more dates because he hated them, after all. He found himself smiling on the way home, enjoying himself despite the fact that they didn't talk. So weird. Beyond anything that he ever thought would have been possible. That was probably why he struggled so much with his decision. Because...he really wanted to see where this relationship would go. Ryland might not be a great conversationalist, but he already knew she was dedicated and loyal, and she was definitely good with kids.

He paid the bill, and they walked out of the restaurant as they always did, quietly, without needing to say anything.

He opened his truck door for her, and she smiled, like she usually did, and nodded her thanks. He nodded back at her and closed the door carefully.

Maybe he could find something to talk about on the way home. He...wanted her to know that he wasn't going to be asking her out again, but it wasn't because he didn't like her or wasn't enjoying what they were doing, even if it was weird.

But as usual, the silence settled between them, and while he didn't feel awkward, it didn't beg to be broken either, and he ended up pulling up in front of her apartment at the back of the library, where the snowdrifts were twice as big as they were on their first date, and jumping out and hurrying around.

He thought maybe she actually waited for him to open her door now, since she seemed to know that he was going to do it. Even though he never said, "Hang on, I'll grab your door." He didn't need to. They'd learned each other without saying anything. He knew she wasn't going to mind if he ate her food, so he didn't worry about it, even though the few people that he'd told had been horrified. And she didn't need him to ask, she just shoved her plate over.

Maybe, maybe sometimes talking got in the way, and he didn't learn as much as what he could have if he had kept his mouth shut to begin with and just paid attention.

It was an intriguing idea, and one he wouldn't have known without Ryland.

He held out his hand. Because of the heat wave they'd been having, where the temperatures had risen to the mid to upper twenties, he wasn't wearing gloves. Neither was she, and her hand was warm and soft in his.

He helped her out and found himself holding onto her fingers, lacing hers with his as he walked her to her apartment. He shouldn't do it. Because he knew he wasn't going to be dating her again. But he couldn't pull his hand away either.

She got the key out of her pocket with her other hand. He held his other hand out, and she set the key in it. It had become their ritual, and again, it happened without words, just things they knew about each other, knew were going to happen, and they didn't need to talk.

Not that words were bad. He certainly didn't think words were bad, he just...thought that maybe he should try silence, too. He...found himself liking it. Or maybe that was just because of Ryland.

He opened her door and handed her key back. This was the point where she started to take it, he didn't let go, and he always asked her on the next date.

There wasn't going to be another date, and he couldn't seem to get any words out of his mouth as they stood there, both of their fingers holding on to her key.

"Do you want to come in?"

He blinked. This wasn't the way things usually went.

"Yes."

The word was out before he even thought about it.

What was he doing? There were going to be no more dates; he was... not exactly breaking up with her, since there wasn't exactly anything going on with her, but he certainly wasn't supposed to be going into her house and...what were they going to do? Sit at the table and stare at each other? Maybe they'd sit on the couch and stare at each other.

Her hand tugged on his as she started walking forward, and he followed her, their linked hands joining them and making it impossible for him to change his mind. Except, he could have opened his mouth and said something.

He saw movement, just as she froze. They stood listening to shouting and yelling down the street.

They turned, despite the night air that was below freezing, to see what was going on.

A mangy dog ran toward them. Three lanky teens were chasing it; two held sticks, and one held something that looked like a can of mace or pepper spray or something.

"Get back here, we're not done with you!" one of the boys called out as they ran, laughing.

The dog was whining and yelping, and it ran straight toward them.

Because Ryland was beside him, his first thought was to put his arm around her and hurry her into her apartment, but before he could do that, she took a step toward the dog and the boys. Her hand slipped out of his, and he was so surprised he didn't move for a couple of seconds. Normal people didn't walk toward danger. Did she know that those kids could be drunk or high or anything in between?

The dog ran past them, and then to his surprise, it turned and cowered behind Ryland's legs.

"It's my dog!" she called, her hands on her hips as the boys seemed to just realize that they had company on the sidewalk. Sweet Water had a tendency to die off completely after seven o'clock, and it was close to eight.

"That's your dog?" one of the boys said.

"It is, Fred, and even if it weren't, you shouldn't be chasing any dogs around Sweet Water."

"You should take better care of your dog," another voice said.

"You're right, Kayden. I should. And I will. But it doesn't matter if I'm not taking care of him, you guys shouldn't be chasing him."

"Sorry, Miss Solomon," the third boy said, looking more guilty than the other two, as he dropped the bat he'd been brandishing and hid it behind him, like putting the weapon out of sight would make everyone forget that he had been holding it in the first place.

"You guys go on back home, or I'm going to be talking to your mothers. All of you know better."

To Lucas's surprise, the boys nodded their heads, looked ashamed, and turned around and started walking away.

He was floored. First of all, Ryland had just uttered more words to those boys then she'd uttered on all four of their dates combined. Second, she hadn't been the slightest bit afraid of them. Third, she'd taken them in hand pretty nicely, and they'd actually seemed...afraid of her, definitely respectful, and like they would do whatever she told them to.

Of course, they'd probably grown up in the library, with their mothers taking them since they were little, and all of them had probably been taught better than what they were doing just then.

Still, he was shocked that Ryland, who had been dating him, had changed into such a different person, and all for the sake of the scrappy-looking canine. Lucas looked around. The dog disappeared.

Ryland watched the boys until they were gone, and then she didn't seem the slightest bit surprised that the dog was nowhere in sight when she turned.

He turned with her, and neither one of them said anything. Him because he couldn't think of anything to say, and her because...he wasn't sure. He would have said that was because that was the way she was, except...was it? Did she turn into a completely different person when he wasn't around?

She moved back to her door without saying anything. "Would you like to come in?"

He'd had plenty of time. He should have come up with something to say, but he hadn't.

Normally he would have. Something along the lines of "Hey, I'd better not go in. This actually has to be our last date. I'm...going to sell myself and probably can't date anyone while I'm doing that."

Nope. That would be way more awkward than any kind of silence, which had actually grown comfortable.

She slipped the lights on, and he closed the door, and they stood inside, her looking over at him for a second before she started taking her hat and coat off.

He paused for just a moment after she pulled her hand away and knew that he should just tell her and then walk back out, but he found himself pulling his hat off and unbuttoning his coat.

"Would you give me kissing lessons?"

He almost swallowed his tongue as he choked and coughed and finally managed to get one word out. "What?"

She stared at him. But didn't repeat her question. She didn't need to, he'd heard her just fine.

She had asked him to give her kissing lessons.

That was the most interesting line he'd ever heard. If he were a guy who tried to use lines, that might be a good one. What woman could resist giving a guy kissing lessons?

What guy could resist giving a woman kissing lessons?

Not him. Not with Ryland, anyway. He certainly didn't want to resist, and he found himself taking one step forward and putting both hands on her shoulders, squeezing, like he was getting ready to comply with her request, standing right there in front of the door with his coat still on.

Except, he couldn't.

"I don't think you want kissing lessons," he said.

"I just asked for them," she pointed out reasonably.

"You want to learn to kiss with your husband. You...don't want to do it with some random dude you might never see again." They lived in a small town. Of course they would see each other again. "Or that you're going to see around town. It would be awkward for us. We kissed and aren't together."

Her eyes narrowed as she stared into his, as though processing that information.

"I'd really like to be with you, but...I can't."

Her brows went up in question. She didn't need to say anything. He could read the questions on her face easily.

He couldn't tell her what he was going to do. It...wasn't something that anyone would think was a reasonable decision on his part, and least of all Ryland, because he would have to explain to her that he really liked her, and she was the reason that it had been difficult for him to come to the conclusion that he had.

But that really wasn't the reason why he didn't want Ryland to have kissing lessons. On the one hand, if he couldn't give them to her, he didn't want her to take them at all, but on the other, she didn't need them. And he didn't need to kiss her to know that.

"I think you feeling like you don't know how to kiss is a good thing. You... Your husband will appreciate the fact that he gets to teach you. I...kind of wish that that would be me. But it's not going to be, and I just think that you won't regret living with what you might feel is a lack of knowledge but is actually...a character thing. Where you haven't kissed every man in town, and your husband isn't walking around wondering whether every man you meet is someone that you kissed before, you know? That...is a priceless gift to give to someone, and I really want your husband to have that."

Her lips had flattened, had maybe turned down slightly at the corners, and it was almost like she loved what he was saying, since her head tilted, and her eyes smiled just a bit.

"If you don't want to kiss me, just say no."

Well, that shot that thought right out of his head. He thought he was getting good at reading her expressions, but he was dead wrong about that one.

"Although, it was kind of nice."

Now he didn't know what to think.

"I wasn't just saying it. I meant it. I... I'd like to, but I know you don't really want me to. Not if I'm not going to stick around, and... I'd really like to, but I just can't."

"Can't is code for don't want to?" She lifted her brows, and he wondered why they couldn't have had a conversation before this. They'd spent four whole dates just staring into each other, and now they were going to talk? Now when he knew he couldn't continue?

"No. Can't actually means can't. I..." He paused. He felt like he could tell her anything. Felt comfortable with her, even though they hadn't talked. But he didn't want to tell her this. Because it was embarrassing.

She'd probably end up hearing about it, but he didn't want to ruin the little bit of time that they had by showing his lack of character. There he was telling her that she would be happier if she didn't kiss a whole lot of men, and here he was, doing something so ridiculously wrong that he could hardly even believe that he was going to do it, and he certainly didn't want to tell anyone.

"I better go. I guess I just wanted to tell you that being with you this past month has been different than anything I've ever done."

She smiled, like she found humor in that. He returned her smile, because he found it funny as well.

"And I know normal people would think I am crazy, but I really enjoyed this time with you. I would be asking you out again, except I can't. And that's not code for anything except I truly can't."

She pressed her lips together and nodded, like she understood, although he knew she didn't. And maybe there was a little bit of hurt in her eyes. He definitely could tell that. But unless he was going to tell her more, that was all she could know.

He moved his thumbs over her shoulders and then made his hands drop.

"Thanks. I'll always remember this time with fondness." And he wouldn't have any regrets, because he hadn't done anything with her that he wouldn't be able to look her future husband in the eye and feel totally okay about. As long as he didn't succumb to the temptation to give her the kissing lesson she'd asked for.

"Thanks. Good luck with your...whatever you're doing," she said.

"Thanks. I'll probably need it. Or something." Since it couldn't be something the Lord was orchestrating. He knew he shouldn't have done it. But it was a sacrifice he made for his family. He kept telling himself that, and maybe someday he wouldn't feel so guilty about it, especially if it ended up saving the ranch as he hoped it would.

He took one more look at her. She might not be classically beautiful, but she just seemed perfect. Perfect for him. If he weren't doing this other thing, he would definitely want to stay tonight, since he'd finally figured out how to talk to her, and do the kissing lessons, and then ask her out, maybe not on a date. Ask her to the farm. She seemed like the kind of person who would be good with animals. And he thought she would really enjoy ranch life.

"Take care," he said as she nodded.

"You too."

Funny how walking away was harder than he expected. Harder than so many other things that he had done. But he opened the door and walked out, wishing that things had turned out differently.

Chapter Six

Ryland waited for the sound of Lucas's truck to fade away before she put her head down on the table.

She knew it. She had known that he wasn't going to stick around. Of course not. Why would he? Fine, it had been more of a blow than what she could have imagined it was going to be. She typically tried to play things cool and didn't have too much of an emotional reaction about things immediately. But this was definitely an exception to that rule.

Then she remembered about the dog.

She'd seen it around most of the winter, but it hadn't let her close to it. She'd put scraps of food out and then around Christmas had actually bought a bag of dog food and a bowl. She left it out at night, and it was gone in the morning, so something was eating it. Although whether or not it was the dog, she wasn't sure. Still, when she saw it, it never let her close to it, and today was the first that it had actually touched her. When it had run behind her and cowered behind her legs, it had brushed against her.

But by the time she was done talking to those boys, the dog had run away.

She honestly wasn't even sure whether it was a boy or girl. She didn't have any idea what kind it was. Something with long hair, and maybe on a good day, it would weigh sixty or seventy pounds.

Still, it wasn't anyone's pet. At least she assumed it wasn't, or else it was badly lost.

There was no humane society in Sweet Water, and the animal control that had jurisdiction was based in Rockerton, she believed. But she kind of wanted to adopt the dog herself, although...she really wasn't any closer to that than what she had been in December when she bought the dog bowl. Maybe she should just call someone and have them try to catch it. If the boys around town were going to be abusing it like that, it would be better off.

Of course, now the whole town was going to think it was hers and that that was the way she treated her dog. She should have thought of something better to say, but the fact that she was able to get words out of her mouth was always a miracle. She couldn't expect them all to come out right. Especially with Lucas beside her.

Lucas.

Well, no more dates. She figured it was coming, but she supposed she should be happy it lasted as long as it did. She definitely hadn't expected that. What kind of guy wanted to go on a date with a woman who didn't talk for four solid dates?

Still, she wished she would have been able to get some words out. For her anyway, the dates would be good memories. He'd eaten her food at all four of them, and she started ordering things that he liked. At least, things that he had ordered before, since she knew she wasn't going to eat.

Of course, what would have happened when she was finally feeling at ease enough to eat while they were out? The poor man would starve to death, if he didn't have her food to eat on top of his.

The thought made her smile, even as she wondered why he had insisted that he couldn't go out with her anymore. Like something was going to happen that was going to make it so that he actually was unable to go out.

Normally she wouldn't have believed that for a second, but he seemed sincere, and she had never heard that he did anything but tell the truth.

She heard some movement outside her door, and she thought that maybe the boys were back for the dog. Sliding back from the table, she opened the door and looked out.

There was nothing. But since she was up, she went over to the side door that opened to the alley and put food in the bowl she kept there. She let the water in the sink run until it was warm, and then she poured it over the top. She tried to make sure she put it out at the same time every evening, because putting the water in the food would make it so that it would freeze if the dog didn't eat it right away, especially on nights where the temps were below zero. At twenty degrees, it would take a little longer, but still, when she was on a routine, she figured that the dog would be able to have some warm food in its belly, even though she couldn't really offer it a place to stay since it wouldn't come to her.

That was why she had told Lucas that she had to be home by eight o'clock.

Of course, it was true that was her bedtime too, or at least the time she started to get ready for bed. It was when she took her shower, brushed her teeth, and got in bed. She might read until midnight, but she was in bed, technically. So she didn't feel like it wasn't the truth.

She smiled a little at what felt like a distant memory now. Bittersweet, because it hadn't worked out the way she wished it would have, but she supposed that was her lot in life and she just ought to be happy with it.

She opened the door, setting the food out and calling, "Come and get it. Supper's ready." Same call she did every night before she stepped back in.

She knew from experience that the dog would not show up until she shut the heavy door, but she could peek out the curtain and watch to make sure it came.

She did that now, and as she stood there, she remembered what she had asked Lucas to do.

She had been so embarrassed and ashamed that she hadn't even been able to think about it. She still felt like crawling under the table when she remembered that she asked for kissing lessons.

Of course he didn't want to give her kissing lessons. He could have kissed her good night any one of the four times he'd taken her out. But he hadn't.

Although, what he said about her not wanting to have kissed every man in town made a lot of sense. Although she hardly doubted her husband would be happy if she was a terrible kisser.

Not that there was any kind of husband anywhere in her near future. That was a definite given.

She saw the dog creep into view, crouching and looking around, before it moved closer to the food.

Every night, it came a little faster, although tonight it was taking a bit longer, maybe because it had been scared by the boys.

If she were home, she would have heard the ruckus and gone out to check, so she didn't think that the boys had been doing that on a regular basis, but now that she knew, she would be keeping an eye out. And their mothers would know about it if she saw them doing it again.

She supposed everyone could make at least one mistake, but if they continuously made the same mistakes over and over again, then there was an issue, and someone needed to step in.

Of course, if it were her, she would want to know immediately if her child was doing something like that. But she didn't think she would let her kid outside running around Sweet Water, without him letting her know exactly what he was doing.

Maybe their mothers thought they knew what their kids were doing.

Ryland wasn't a mom, and she supposed she had a lot to learn.

Thinking of moms, her thoughts went to her own mother, who had raised her by herself.

At least until Ryland was twelve. Then she'd remarried and started a family with her new husband. Ryland had never felt like she quite fit in, although her stepdad had been...kind, if not exactly fatherly toward her.

Still, when her great aunt had passed away, and Ryland had inherited her estate, she answered the ad for a librarian in the town of Sweet Water, even though the pay was low. With the inheritance, she could afford to accept the low pay, and it wasn't like she was trying to support a family. Or buy a house. As long as she was content with her apartment, and she was, she really didn't need much.

She supposed if she did end up adopting the dog, it would be an additional expense, but...she felt like maybe the companionship might be worth it. She wasn't lonely, not really, but on a night like tonight, when she'd basically been dumped by the guy that she'd been dating, no matter how casually or awkwardly it was, she could have used a furry companion to tell her troubles to.

She wanted to wait for a little bit, thinking that she might go out and see if the dog would let her walk up to it, but then she decided to stick with her original plan of waiting until it was warmer out, and it wouldn't be such a huge deal if it missed a meal, leaving and not coming back.

With a last look, she turned, feelings of embarrassment and sadness still swirling through her, and headed toward the other side of her apartment where her bedroom and bathroom were.

She would definitely be reading a book for a long time tonight before she felt the slightest bit tired and could possibly think about sleeping.

The next time someone asked her out on a date, she was going to say no.

<h1 style="text-align:center">Chapter Seven</h1>

"You're going to do what?" Ada asked as the entire room went silent.

Lucas had figured that the best time for him to make his announcement to his family would be after their Sunday afternoon dinner. But even for an extrovert like himself, it was a little bit intimidating. After all, he had eleven siblings, and every one of them except for Lois was there.

Plus, now that Ezra and Asher and Claudia were married, their spouses were with them. Alaska had come with two children, so there was that as well, plus Mina was still with Claudia, And of course, Joanna's best friend, Stonewall, was there as well. He was almost a part of the family since he had moved from Wyoming to North Dakota with them and worked just as hard as the rest of the family.

Everyone figured that eventually Joanna and Stonewall would end up married, but Joanna in particular seemed to be completely oblivious to how good things could be between her and Stonewall, seeing him only as a friend and absolutely nothing more. She seemed to have a one-track mind and a single-minded focus, and it was all about saving the ranch.

They were still young, though.

Which it was funny that Lucas would even think that, since Joanna was only six years younger than him. But he felt worlds older, especially now that he made this decision.

"Is that even a thing?" Caleb asked, his head on his hand as he smashed his face up, as though he were searching his brain to try to figure out if he'd ever heard of anything like this happening.

"You can find a lot of things for sale on the deep web."

"The deep web?" Phoebe asked softly. Of all the siblings, Phoebe was probably the most innocent, although she was the oldest girl and second only to Ezra in birth order.

"I'm not going to explain to you about the deep web right now, just know that there are a lot of illegal things that go on, and you can pretty much find anyone to do anything. This was a way I found to make money, and I jumped on it."

"Wait. You're not doing this because you want to, you're doing it to...make money?" Asher scratched his head and then exchanged a look with his wife, Sondra.

"Have we decided exactly what it is that he's doing?" Priscilla said, giving Lucas a look like only an older sister could.

"He's not doing it." Ezra's voice was firm as he sat at the head of the table, staring down at Lucas, with a look on his face that was so close to the way their dad used to look at him that Lucas almost agreed with him immediately.

He turned to Ada, figuring that he should answer her question first. "I said I'm going to sell myself to the highest bidder and get married to her."

"Is that even a thing?" Ada responded, like they were the only two in the room, and he could see the concern and worry in her eyes. After all, she was his older sister, by just two years, but she cared about him, and while he'd done some pretty crazy things over his lifetime, this definitely took the cake.

"It must be a thing if he's doing it. But I say no."

"Sorry, Caleb. But you don't have veto power over my life. I'm more than old enough to make my own decisions, the ranch needs the money, and this seemed like a good idea. So, I'm gonna do it." His stomach felt like it held balled-up barbed wire, but he tried not to let that show on his face.

"This just feels like a spur-of-the-moment decision. Surely we can come up with something else," Claudia said, biting her lip.

Claudia was probably the sister he was the closest to, and he gave her a reassuring smile. "I know I have a reputation for doing things on the spur of the moment, but trust me, I thought long and hard about this."

"When you say long and hard, you mean you thought about it for almost five minutes." Asher definitely knew him.

"I thought about it for a week before I put my application in."

"Yeah. A week. You made a decision that's going to change the rest of your life, change our lives, change everything we are, in a week?" Priscilla might as well have her hands on her hips or be pointing her finger at him like a schoolmarm.

"That's a long time for me." He said it flippantly, but he really had thought about it. "The family needs it. I'm available, and I'm willing. I figure it'll be a sacrifice, at the very most. Maybe I'll end up with someone that I really like. Regardless, I'll get the money, the ranch will be carried through until spring when we can sell our weaners and we'll have finished steers to put on the market as well. Hopefully we'll start getting more dude ranch business. The timing couldn't be better."

"Except you're selling yourself to the highest bidder. And you don't know who that will be."

"That's true. But...I'm just not worried about it."

"What kind of woman is so desperate to get married that she's going to bid on someone on an online auction?" Caleb asked and shook his head.

"You might be surprised about that," Priscilla said, and there was some humor in her tone. It was enough to break the tension of the table, and they all laughed.

"Women can be pretty desperate," Ada agreed. It was funny, that neither one of those two were married, and they were talking about how desperate women could be. He hoped that they weren't thinking of anything this crazy. He would be really upset if they were, and he could understand how the rest of his siblings would be upset with him.

"The ranch is not in such bad shape that we need you to sacrifice the rest of your life in order to save it. If we lose it, we lose it. We're all quite capable of getting jobs off the ranch. In fact, some of us are more suitable to be working off the ranch. We'll just assume that that's what the Lord has for us, and we'll pick up the pieces and follow His plan."

Ezra made a lot of sense, as he always did, but he also sounded a little bit desperate, like he'd already figured out that Lucas was determined to go through with this, and it didn't matter what anyone said.

"Maybe God's plan is that I put myself up for auction, and we keep the ranch."

Ezra's lips flattened, as though that was not a viable statement at all, in any way.

"What could you possibly have been thinking?" Phoebe asked, shaking her head.

He and Phoebe were probably as opposite as any of the siblings were. He was outgoing and vivacious, willing to take risks, and loved challenges, but was a true dreamer, whereas Phoebe was quiet and soft and sweet and fiercely loyal, but also very much a pragmatist.

"I was thinking that instead of all of us going down with the ranch, one of us would make a sacrifice, and the rest of us would be able to benefit from that sacrifice. I'm confident that it's not going to be a terrible thing, but even if it is, I am willing to do it to keep everyone else together." He said that as firmly as he could. That was where his thought process had been.

He wanted to do this, make that sacrifice for his siblings. It was a sacrifice for his family, and to him, nothing was too great to sacrifice for the people he loved, and there was no one in this world that he loved more than his family.

Maybe he could have loved Ryland like that, but thankfully, things had not progressed to that point. Maybe that was why the Lord had kept them from talking on their dates at all. Maybe he would have fallen head over heels and not been able to make the sacrifice.

"I still don't understand how you even figured out there was such a thing?" Caleb just couldn't let that go. He had to figure out how things work. Tobias was sitting beside him, shaking his head. Of all of them, Tobias was the one who was able to fix things. He worked with his hands, and it wasn't surprising that he hadn't said a thing so far the whole conversation.

Actually, of all of his siblings, Lucas expected Tobias would be the one who would support him. Tobias was probably wondering why he hadn't thought of it first.

"I thought of the deep web. It's someplace I ended up because I was looking for things that...were honest but maybe a little bit shady. You have to be willing to take risks if you want a big payoff, and I wanted a huge payoff, because that's what we needed." He lifted a shoulder. "So, this looked intriguing. It would give me the money I need, and I mean, there were other options where I wouldn't actually get married. You just ended up being a slave to whoever bought you, and...I didn't want to end up doing something that was inappropriate. Marriage seemed like the best idea."

"I see," Ezra said, one hand moving over the stubble on his face. Lucas thought that was the one redeeming aspect of this whole thing, and Ezra had figured that out. He could have been sold to someone and not marry them. They could have...done whatever they wanted to with him.

"I don't understand how that's going to work." Tobias spoke, and his voice sounded calm and rational, like he was coming around. Lucas figured he would be the first one on board. If he could get this right, everyone else could go in after. Tobias was a bit of a leader, even though he was number five in birth order. He was going to do this whether his siblings agreed with him or not, but it would make it a lot easier if they were all on board.

"The auction is already going on. People have already bid on me. So, I know that from the picture and description I've given them, they like what they see."

"What is that exactly?" Ada asked, wrinkling up her nose.

"I gave them a picture, my bio. I went to my social media profiles, and I uploaded some pictures of our ranch and the story of our family. They can link to a couple of articles about our parents, and so they can see that that part is true. And I did mention the financial difficulty on the ranch, but I would think it will be obvious from what I've said that that was the motivation behind this. Making money for the ranch."

"I see. But I still don't understand about the auction," Asher said.

"They can bid now, but the auction is going to end at the courthouse steps in Rockerton. Whoever buys me is going to go in immediately, get a license, and get married. That way, it's done and over with. We'll also have a legal document that will be filled out that will say I am tied to them for at least five years."

"You can't even get divorced if she cheats on you?"

"No. I mean, I can probably get a lawyer and pay my way out of it, but...I've got five years at least. And it's a marriage, so I'm looking at it as a lifetime commitment."

"But you might be getting married to someone who doesn't look at it that way." Asher's statement was flat.

"I know. It's a risk. It's a chance I have to take, but the payoff is huge. The payoff being we can keep the ranch. We won't be pressed against the wall for the rest of the spring, and Ezra, you've already aged so much in the last year." He looked around the table, and the siblings all nodded their heads. "The stress has been wearing on you. I mean, Alaska has been the best thing that's ever happened to you, but the stress of running the ranch, of making this thing work, of knowing that there are people who are depending on you on all sides, it has to be hard. This is a way that will take some of that stress and transfer it to me."

"No stress is being transferred to you; it's a ball and chain. And that could be a literal ball and chain," Claudia said, and she was truly concerned.

"I understand where you're coming from. I think it probably isn't the wisest thing you've ever done, but...I like it. Willing to sacrifice for your family. That shows character. You need credit for that." Tobias spoke, and the entire table was silent.

Lucas wanted to fist pump the air, but he figured that would break the atmosphere that had descended. Everyone respected Tobias. Almost as much as they respected Ezra, and if he said that this would be an okay idea, that it would work, that it was something that they should admire, it made them pause. And consider. Think about how he might possibly be right.

"Tobias." Ezra didn't need to say anything more, but it wasn't a reprimand so much as it was an exclamation of shock.

Tobias looked coolly at his older brother and lifted his brows. "Am I wrong?"

Ezra's lips pressed together. It was obvious that he was thinking about what Tobias had said, and he finally shook his head. "I hate it. I hate the idea that somebody would sacrifice so much, but...you're right. It shows character and integrity and a willingness to put others first that most people could never even dream about."

After that, Lucas allowed himself a self-satisfied smile. He was scared to death, if he was being honest. Which he wouldn't admit to anyone. Not any of the siblings anyway. For some reason, Ryland's face came into his head, and he thought maybe he could admit it to her. Except, that was laughable because he couldn't even talk to her, let alone admit his deepest, darkest thoughts and feelings.

"But he could ruin the rest of his life!" Priscilla insisted.

"Not ruin, sacrifice. There's a difference. A deliberate choice that you know is going to potentially be harmful to yourself, but is going to benefit everyone around you, is not necessarily a ruination of you. It could actually help you to grow even stronger character, although that kind of choice means you have a strong character to begin with." Tobias spoke with authority, and even though he was younger than Priscilla and she narrowed her eyes at him, she kept her mouth closed and seemed to be thinking about what he had just said.

Lucas couldn't have said it better. And he might not even have articulated all of that to himself. He just knew that he had the means to save the family, even though it meant potentially not having the life he thought he was going to have. But wasn't he supposed to give his life to the Lord anyway? It wasn't supposed to be about living for himself. It wasn't supposed to be about making sure that he was as comfortable and happy as he could possibly be and being unwilling to give anything for anyone else. But following God, and doing what God wanted, being willing to give up, sacrifice, for the people he loved.

"I just hope she appreciates you." Tobias lifted his brows at Lucas, and those words meant more than an effusive declaration of congratulations from anyone else.

Lucas grinned and made it the carefree, easygoing grin that his family was used to. "I'll make sure she does."

He had no idea whether he could do any such thing. The bidding online showed him that people had bid, but he couldn't see their names or enough information to look them up and to see what he was getting into. But he had a tendency to think that anyone who was going to be bidding on someone, to marry them, probably wasn't going to be the ideal wife.

But he was confident this was the way he was supposed to go. While he didn't necessarily think that this was the way that God was going to work for everyone, it was obvious that the Lord had opened the door, and he was going to walk through it, even though it was scary and hard. It would be worth it, to know that his siblings were safe on the ranch, and he was the only one who might potentially not be around. Which was sad but still worth it.

"When does the auction end?" Phoebe asked, and while she was sweet and quiet, she was also probably the most intelligent one of all the siblings. The one who was able to take information in, assimilate it, and come out with important conclusions, knowing how to ask the right questions.

"Saturday."

"That's just six days away!"

"Yep. Although, I wouldn't want it to drag on. I'm glad it's not going to be a long time. If... If I'm going to do it, I want to move on."

His brothers nodded, but his sisters didn't seem so sure. He figured that was probably one of those things that were male-female differences. It didn't matter. Other than he had five days left with his siblings.

"Well, I suppose since you only have a limited time left with us, we better get all the work out of you that we can. So, let's plan our week."

Everyone laughed. Lucas figured Ezra was mostly joking. He would probably deliberately plan several days off so they had some extra time to spend together, although it was winter, and typically they weren't doing anything more than what they had to, other than servicing the equipment that they would need for spring planting.

As for him, he was going to enjoy these last five days, because they were not just the last days he got to spend with his family, but they were the last days he would spend not married.

Ryland's request that he teach her how to kiss went through his mind. He had five days while that was still an option, although he knew he had done the right thing by turning her down. He hadn't wanted to, and he was afraid that he might hurt her feelings. But he knew what he had told her was right. She should let her husband teach her how to kiss. He only wished that it would have been him.

Chapter Eight

"Oh my goodness. That smells delicious," Agathe said as she lifted the lid of the crockpot that Ryland Solomon had just brought in.

"It's a little thing called Mississippi Pot Roast. It was on one of the library sites online, and it looked so good I had to try it. I've been making it ever since."

"I can see why. This just smells absolutely amazing. If it tastes even half that good, it's going to be delicious."

"I think it tastes better than it smells, but my opinion might be a little biased."

Ryland was such a sweetheart, with her quiet ways and her ability to blend in the background but still see what needed to be done and step up and volunteer.

Agathe had enjoyed the meals that she had made for her over the last month or so, almost on a weekly basis. She especially appreciated the fact that Ryland had offered to stay with Jim more than once, since they switched the day of the Alzheimer's support group from Saturday to Tuesday. Tuesday was the day that Ryland often brought her meal. The library closed early on Tuesdays and didn't open on Wednesday until dinnertime. Ryland had explained that gave her extra time to do something, and she might as well make a meal and sit with Jim.

Agathe didn't think that Ryland probably enjoyed the sports channel on TV at all, but she typically read a book on her Kindle app on her phone and seemed quite content.

Of course, Jim had not done anything wild or crazy while Ryland was there. Several people had been scared away when Jim had gone through one of his spells where he didn't know anyone and didn't even seem to know himself or the common rules of decency. Twice, she found him outside without his clothes on, and once, when someone had been watching him, he had tried to do the same. That person hadn't been back.

It wasn't like Jim could help it, and there wasn't anything Agathe could do either.

"Are you sure you're okay with him?" she asked.

"We'll be just fine," Ryland said.

Agathe had left Jim in front of the TV. He was in one of his states where he didn't know anyone, and she wasn't even going to go in and say goodbye to him. He wouldn't know her and would be upset that she was even talking to him. She didn't know how people dealt with this without TVs, since that had been the best babysitter she'd been able to find.

As long as he was watching sports, he was typically okay, although hockey didn't really interest him at all. So if there was a hockey game on, that's when she was most likely to have trouble.

"I'll be back by nine o'clock," she said, smiling at Ryland after she gave her a few other instructions.

Ryland waved her hand. "Take your time. If you want to go for ice cream or something afterward with some of the other people, you know that's fine. I have someone feeding my dog, so I can be out as late as you need."

"I hardly think I'll do that, but if I do, I will definitely let you know, okay?"

"That's fine. I just have to be back to the library tomorrow at noon."

She definitely wasn't going to be out overnight. Although... She thought again of Waylen at the support group. He had become a good friend. She...found herself deliberately choosing a chair beside him if she came in after he did. She'd gotten there early several times, and he had taken a look at the mostly empty chairs and then deliberately come over and sat down beside her.

Even though he lost his wife from Alzheimer's, and it had been over a year since she passed, he was still coming to the meetings. She...would be sad when he stopped.

It didn't take long to drive there, and she got out, bringing the notebook that she'd taken to carrying around with her. Every once in a while, the support group leader would say something that she wanted to try to remember. Things like, *remember the good times, appreciate the times when he knows who you are. Just focus on one day at a time. Don't try to look down the road and think of all the things that are going to happen. That's too overwhelming.* She really emphasized how important it was to take breaks and also to keep her mind focused on happy things.

Of course, being a support group leader, she also focused on how important it was to maintain friendships and get out a little, spending time with people who understood and, preferably, with people who had been there themselves.

The support group leader practically encouraged her to do something with Waylen.

When she arrived, there were already four people there. Waylen had not arrived. She took a seat and got her notebook out, writing the date at the top and thinking about whether there was anything she wanted specifically to address. Sometimes during the week, she would come up with questions that she wanted to talk to the other folks in the circle about. Sometimes it was just helpful to get someone else's perspective on things.

She had just remembered that she wanted to ask about door locks. One time two weeks ago, Jim had gone outside, and the weather had been well below zero. She happened to wake up when he opened the door, but what if she hadn't? Surely there were locks that they could put on doors that would keep the doors from being opened unless she was there supervising. Maybe locks that were remote controlled or something. She wasn't sure.

"Hey there. I think every time I see you, you look younger and prettier."

She laughed up at Waylen. He had a way of talking to her that made her feel like a young girl again, instead of an old woman facing her retirement years and taking care of a husband who didn't know who she was anymore.

"Waylen. It's so good to see you," she said, trying not to giggle like a schoolgirl.

"Is this seat taken?" he asked, indicating the chair beside her. He hadn't started to sit down in it, and she could absolutely say yes, if she wanted to. After all, she had often wondered if maybe her feelings for Waylen were...crossing some kind of line. She definitely thought about him when she wasn't in the support group.

"No. Please sit down."

She really enjoyed his company, and he did lift her spirits. And he was a good man. Faithful to his wife, and faithful to the support group. He never missed a meeting. Even if it was well below zero. He also was known to be active for his age, physically anyway, even though she knew he was several years older than she was. She liked that he still got out and did things.

"So, I was wondering if you might be interested in going for a cup of hot chocolate after we're done here?" He lifted up his hands. "Don't feel like you have to. And it's only a friendship thing, of course. Just... I know how hard it can be when you're stuck at home all the time, especially in these North Dakota winters. Just something fun to get out for a bit. No pressure."

She was going to say no, but then he added that last bit, and she found herself nodding and saying, "I'd love to. You're right. Sometimes I go a little stir-crazy because I can't really leave him, because I'm afraid he'll try to go outside. He doesn't like to get out like I do. I just need sunshine sometimes."

"Yeah. I totally know how that goes. The last couple of years that my wife was home, I couldn't leave her alone for even a minute." He sighed, and his eyes got a faraway look in them. "It was tough. Sometimes I couldn't make it to the meeting if I didn't have someone to watch her. She... It was just hard to see her like that. She had always been so alive, so funny, so desperately in love with me." He laughed a little, like it was funny to say, or maybe it didn't sound humble to him, but it was the truth.

Agathe could see how it would be. He seemed like such a nice guy. How could his wife not love him?

He shook his head. "She still kept her personality. Even if she had no clue who I was. It just hurt, you know?" His eyes squinted a little bit.

"Yeah. Boy, I can really relate to that." It didn't surprise her. He'd been through it all, and he totally understood what she was going through. She could have said the same thing, word for word. That it hurt when her husband didn't know her, and his personality really hadn't changed too much, other than the odd things he did, like walk outside in the middle of the night in nothing but his underwear and bedroom slippers, or how upset he got when he didn't know where he was or who she was.

"I guess Jim's personality has changed a little. He didn't used to get upset over anything. But maybe he really was upset and just good at hiding it." She'd thought of that too. That maybe he had been upset more than he let on, and he was just able to control himself so that he didn't show her his temper. She supposed she did that at times, where she was irritated, but she didn't want to be, so she didn't allow the people around her to be affected by her irritation.

"That might be. My wife was just...always sweet. I don't know that she ever got irritated, but I think the disease almost made her better. Where she didn't even notice the things that might have bothered her before. I don't know. It's just... I just understand how hard it is. And it doesn't really get easier. Not until...it's over. And that of course has its own problems and trials."

"I haven't even gotten to that point. I don't know if I can handle it if I allow myself to remember that it gets harder."

"It's the loneliness. You know, you miss them, you want them, nobody quite fills in the gap the way they did. But still, an empty house is just sad." He smiled. "Now you know I want to go out for hot chocolate just as much for myself as I do for you."

"Well, if that makes you feel better. I would hate to think it was all about me, and it's really nice to know that even in what feels like a state of inability to do anything besides take care of myself and my husband, that maybe I'm shining a little bit of a light in someone else's life."

"You definitely are. I look forward to coming every week, not just because it gets me out of the house, and I don't have to listen to the silence pushing in from all directions, but also because sometimes it's just lonely being alone."

"I bet it would be," she said, thinking that was rather brave of him to admit that. It was definitely something she hadn't thought about. She hadn't gotten to that point. She was still thinking about how much she missed the Jim she knew. That she'd fallen in love with. The man who had been her rock throughout her marriage, and now she felt like she was more adrift than ever.

But in a way that was good as well, because she felt like she relied more on the Lord than she ever had. And it had definitely shown her where she had relied on her husband rather than God to take care of her. Which wasn't necessarily a terrible thing. God gave a person their spouse so they didn't have to walk through life alone, so that together they could be more than the sum of both of them, but...sometimes having a spouse became an idol, she supposed.

The meeting went by quickly, although Agathe found herself having trouble paying attention. She didn't want to think it was because she was going out on a date with Waylen. It wasn't a date, right? It was...just two friends getting together.

Except, she liked the way he made her feel young again. Not necessarily young in age, just young in mind. Because the cares of her life had been weighing down so hard, the worries about Jim, his health issues, and all the pain and suffering that came from having a husband who was no longer a husband but more like a child that she had to take care of, a big, heavy baby who needed twenty-four-hours-a-day, seven-days-a-week care.

As they packed up to leave, Waylen said, "I'd really like to drive you there, but I suppose we should just take our vehicles separately. That way, we won't have to come back for them."

"Yeah. That makes sense." And it made it seem less like a date if they drove separately. But she didn't say that, because he hadn't done anything that had been crossing the line of friendship. He was just giving her a shoulder to lean on. That was all.

Thankfully, the ice-cream shop in Sweet Water was still open when they got there, and hot chocolate was on special.

It was less than five dollars later that they were sitting at a booth together, each with a steaming mug in front of them.

"My insulin numbers are going to be out of this world. I probably shouldn't drink this," he said.

"I think they have a sugar-free version," Agathe said, although perhaps she should have gotten it as well. She wasn't getting out nearly like she used to, taking walks along the mostly deserted roads early in the morning. Even in the winter, she would get out a little, shovel some snow, play with her dog, which they'd lost several years prior, and she just hadn't felt like she could get another one after Jim's diagnosis. A puppy took a lot of care, and she didn't have the mental bandwidth. She thought one more mess every day might be more than she could handle.

"I'll keep that in mind for next time. Maybe we can make this a thing, coming for hot chocolate after the support group."

"Maybe," she said, smiling into his eyes but knowing she probably ought not to do such a thing. It was one thing to go out once in a while, it was another thing to make it a regular thing, just the two of them. It was too much like...like they were becoming a couple. She needed to be careful.

Of course, she told herself that maybe she ought not to worry about it. It wasn't like she was in danger of falling in love and leaving her husband or anything. And just like she didn't have time for a dog or time for her walks anymore, she certainly didn't have time to handle a new romantic relationship. Even if that was something she was considering, which she wasn't. Jim was not gone.

Although, part of her argued that he actually *was* gone. The Jim she knew anyway.

"So you're from France originally?" Waylen said as he used his spoon to take a little bite of the whipped cream that sat on top of his hot chocolate.

She did the same, since it was too hot to drink.

"Yes. Jim was in the service, and he was stationed in Germany. We met when he and his friends were on holiday, touring the French countryside. I think it was love at first sight, and he spent every chance he could get away with me. He was so dashing and kind, loved my family, and my mother actually approved of him, even though he was an American. I think she knew he would probably take me away, although at the time, I was so young and innocent that it never occurred to me that in order to be with him, I would have to leave my home. My family. And never see them again. Or just occasionally. Jim and I were going to go back last summer, but he got so bad that I knew a trip would be impossible."

"I've always wanted to see France. I'm a bit of a history buff, loving World War II in particular. I'd love to see the beaches of Normandy and the graveyards of American soldiers. I've seen pictures, but it just would be really neat to be able to go see them for myself."

"Oh, I think they're amazing! You really need to go. It's beautiful. The whole country of France is just brimming with things to see. I think people often think of Paris when they think of France, and they're missing so much."

"Well, I guess if I make it, I'll definitely have to consult you for my itinerary, although I don't think I would like to go alone. I don't speak French."

"Oh my goodness. It's been so long since I was able to converse in my native tongue. But I don't think it really matters. There are so many people in France who know English, and we're all eager to practice, so it wouldn't be hard at all for you to get around that language barrier."

"But it would be easier if I had my own interpreter."

"I suppose it would be."

"Maybe we'll do that someday. Go to France together." He spoke casually, then blew on his hot chocolate and took a sip. "It's cool enough to drink now, if you're careful."

She nodded and lifted her cup up, but she was kind of stunned at what he had said. She wanted to go back to her home country so much, and...he wanted to go see it too. Maybe the trip that she had been longing for would still be possible.

Not with Jim, of course. And that made her excitement dim, because Jim was the one that she always wanted to do everything with.

The only one. He was the one she had a good time with, the one she was comfortable with, the one she could let her hair down with and knew that he would not only take care of her, but he would love her no matter what. They just...fit together so well.

But maybe it was something to look forward to. Something to think about when Jim wasn't with her anymore. There was someone else who was willing to do some of the things she was interested in. And the idea that her trip might still happen was...exciting.

They chatted about the weather, which was something that everyone always talked about, and how cold it had been, and she told him about acclimating to the North Dakota cold when she and Jim had first moved. He had laughed, because as a native of North Dakota, he had grown up here, and while temperatures of minus twenty and minus thirty were never comfortable for anyone, he took them as a matter of course.

He seemed sturdy and hearty and dependable, and she found a lot to admire in him and found herself sad when it was time for them to go. It seemed like next Tuesday was a world away, and she had a whole week of heartbreak and hard work and loneliness... He was so right about the loneliness. Because Jim really wasn't with her. She was mostly alone with a stranger. That was all she had to look forward to until next Tuesday. When she would get to go and have hot chocolate with Waylen again.

She found herself looking forward to it. Probably more than she should have.

Chapter Nine

"Are you really going to read all of these books this week, Vince?" Ryland said as the serious ten-year-old set a stack of very adult-looking books on her desk.

"A couple of them are for my mom, but I like to read too," he said, and the way he talked reminded her so much of herself. Like he was talking because he was forced to and not necessarily because he enjoyed conversing with other people.

His eyes were cast down, and while sometimes that could mean a person wasn't honest or upright, it could also mean that eye contact was painful for them, the way it often was for her. She had worked hard on being able to look people in the eye when she spoke to them. One of the things she often asked herself after she spoke with someone was what color their eyes were as she walked away. If she didn't know, then she knew that she hadn't been successful in her goal to meet their eyes and make eye contact.

Of course, she knew exactly what color eyes Lucas had.

She laughed to herself. He'd broken up with her a week and a half ago, and she was still thinking about him. And his eyes. Apparently.

"Well, I think we're going to have good reading weather next week." They were supposed to get a bit of warm weather. And the temperatures might even poke up above freezing on Saturday, but the next week was supposed to be blustery and the temperatures were going to be the coldest they'd been all winter.

Which was saying something. But for herself, Ryland was looking forward to it. It was perfect reading weather, like she just told Vince.

He nodded and seemed eager to leave, as he shifted from one foot to the other.

"All right, when you bring them back, you have to let me know what you thought. I haven't read this one yet." She tapped the book on top.

"I'm excited about it. I think it's going to be really good," he said, and there was excitement in his voice, although his words were a little choppy, like he was pushing them out.

Again, she could understand and hoped that he was able to work on the issues that he had, the same as she had.

Of course, she was the way God made her, and insinuating that there was something wrong with her was an insult to her creator. But the fact of the matter was, it was much easier to get along in society if a person at least appeared a little bit more normal on the surface.

Why couldn't she talk to Lucas? She would have loved to look normal on the surface with him. Typically, she wasn't a huge talker, but it wasn't like she was mute for hours on end in someone's company, either. At least not typically.

But there was nothing about her feelings for Lucas that were typical. Except for possibly the fact that she couldn't seem to get over him.

The rest of the afternoon was busy as it seemed like most people had the same idea she did—next week was going to be a really great week to read.

There were winter activities that North Dakotans enjoyed, including ice hockey and skiing, and while there weren't too many hills in North Dakota, when the snow came down, sometimes kids would grab their sleds, and hook onto the back of a bumper of a car, and fly down the street that way.

Other times, they would slide down drifts that formed in the wind or make their own hills out of snow.

Kids were just as adaptable and creative today as they had been when she was growing up.

Of course, there would be a subset who would be inside watching TV or on their electronics. She supposed that worked for them, but it made her a little bit sad, because she felt like they were missing out. But that was just her opinion, and obviously as a librarian, she would feel that way about books as well as the outside activities.

Still, by the time she had bid the last person goodbye and turned off the lights in the library section of the building, she was looking forward to grabbing a bite of supper and snuggling under the covers with a good book.

She still had two hours until it was time for her to feed...not *her* dog, but *the* dog. She needed to think of a good name for him too. Sweetie just wasn't cutting it, although she probably ought to figure out whether it was a boy or girl before she gave it a name that was wildly inappropriate.

She put on her snuggly jammies and her big fluffy rabbit flippers and had come out to make a cup of tea to take back into her bedroom with her when there was a knock at the door.

It wasn't that late in the evening, but she never had visitors after the library closed. If someone wanted to see her, they almost always came while it was open, except for a few friends, who might stop in when they were in town, especially on the weekend.

Possibly on Tuesday afternoon when they knew the library was closed.

She wasn't terribly concerned while she walked to the door, since she had just talked to her mom a couple of days before and everything was fine. She supposed she would like to have a closer relationship with her mom, but when she spoke with her on the telephone, she had a tendency to go on about the issues that she was having with her children and her life now, which didn't seem to resemble anything that Ryland remembered and didn't include Ryland at all.

They had struggled a lot for money, and they had lived in a lot of one-bedroom apartments on the shady side of town.

Now her mom lived in a nice, comfortable middle-class home in the suburbs of Raleigh, North Carolina. There really wasn't anything similar in the children that she had now who had a dad living with them, who cared about them and wanted the best for them. Her mom had a relationship that, while it wasn't perfect, it was good and solid and made her mom happy.

Yeah, Ryland really couldn't think of very many similarities to her own childhood. It was almost like it never existed. That she was the mistake that her mom had before she settled into a really good life. She knew her mom didn't see her like that, but that was just the way she felt sometimes.

She was deep in thought as she opened the door, and it took her a minute to recognize the person standing on her stoop. It was freezing out, and the wind blew hard, whipping the snow around, so she couldn't tell whether there was more snow coming down or whether that was the snow that was already there just being driven in great gusts with the wind.

"Lucas?"

"I was wondering if you wanted to go out on one last date?"

Chapter Ten

Lucas couldn't believe he was standing here on Ryland's step, asking for one last date.

He knew there was no future for them, and he had always been a big believer in dating being practice for divorce. He hadn't done it much, and he had been even a bigger believer in not dating around. Since that was even more practice for divorce.

His family had taught that dating wasn't very good practice for marriage anyway. It was better to spend time with the person doing regular things, rather than spending a lot of time on one's best behavior, at a place that one didn't typically visit. It certainly didn't give a very good slice of life or let them know how someone acted in everyday situations. You only saw how they acted when they were on their best behavior when all circumstances around them were perfect.

Whereas, if he had someone he was interested in and invited them over to spend time with family, especially a family like his, he was very much likely to see their true personality, and how they rubbed along with things that didn't go their way, or how they got along with people who didn't do what they wanted them to, or didn't act the way they thought they should, or had personalities that clashed with theirs.

Not that he felt like it was okay to deliberately put people through a trial by fire, but that was pretty much what it was when someone visited their family.

He could see the wisdom there and see that he would get a truer sense of a person's character, without developing feelings that were potentially going to be difficult to get over, when he found out that the person that he was dating wasn't exactly what he wanted. By then, he was too deeply invested to call the relationship what it was and move on.

He had done everything wrong with Ryland. Except, he'd already seen her at work. He spent a lot of time watching her with the kids at the library and knew her from around town. He...had always liked what he saw, and he supposed that his fear of being so emotionally attached that he didn't want to let go had actually come true.

He was getting married tomorrow to the highest bidder, and he wanted one last date with Ryland tonight. His family had wanted to do something together, but he had talked them into doing something tomorrow morning. He said it would help the morning pass faster, since he would be nervous, and that had given him tonight to go to the library.

Then, he realized how ridiculous he was being, because it was already six thirty, and she didn't like to be out late. She said she went to bed at eight o'clock, and they couldn't make it to Rockerton and back... But they could make it to the diner. They would have something good, and maybe that would be almost as nice?

It just didn't seem...good enough for her. Good enough for their last date, good enough for...what he wanted.

"Oh! Come on in. It's freezing out there."

He stepped in, and she closed the door behind him.

The issue that he had with his mouth not working took hold of him again. Why did this happen every time he saw her?

He had even practiced in the mirror at home, something he had never had to do before. Wanting to make this last evening with her perfect. Although he didn't know why. He shouldn't be thinking about her when he was going to be marrying someone else tomorrow. Except, he didn't know who it was, most likely had not even met her yet, and all he could think about was that he wished it was Ryland.

But he knew she couldn't afford him on her small librarian salary.

And he wasn't regretting what he had decided to do. He knew that the sacrifice for his family would be worth it; he just...probably would always wonder what might have been between him and Ryland. Because, once he was married tomorrow, he had no plans on ever walking away from his marriage. Even though he would technically, according to the contract he was going to sign, be free in five years. Marriage was marriage, and it was forever.

He took a deep breath and reminded himself that this was his last chance. If he didn't talk to her now, he might never talk to her again.

That might have been a little bit dramatic, but he could never talk to her again the way he wanted to talk to her tonight.

The only thing that almost kept him from coming was the idea that she might ask him to teach her how to kiss again, and if she did... He wasn't sure he could turn her down a second time.

He wasn't even sure he would be able to go for the whole evening without asking her if she still wanted him to do it, because he was more than willing to give her a lesson.

A part of him said, why not? After all, he wasn't married, wasn't engaged, and wasn't attached in any way, and neither was she. A kiss wouldn't hurt anything. It certainly wasn't prohibited by the Bible, although...it just seemed smart to refrain from kissing anyone that a person wasn't married to, since kissing was designed to lead to more. To things that were directly forbidden by the Bible and things that were expressly for the sole enjoyment of a married couple.

Still, he decided to take a chance. He knew his reasoning was faulty, but he figured this was the last thing he was going to do for himself for a very long time. It...wasn't the smartest thing he'd ever done, but he was giving up a lot, and he thought that maybe one last date with Ryland was one thing that he could give to himself, since he was sacrificing so much. It would be the one last thing in a very long time that he did for himself.

And while he had prayed about it, he wasn't entirely sure that God was giving him the green light, or whether he just wanted to see it, so he did. Regardless, he had every intention of trying to just keep it to what they had done before. Except, he'd like it if they could talk a little this time. Although, he wasn't even sure he needed that. The silences with

Ryland were just fine. They...somehow were almost as good as talking if that was possible.

But as he looked at her, he realized she was dressed for bed.

"I had...intended to take you out, but you look like you're ready for bed." She hadn't answered him when he asked if she wanted to go on a date, and now he felt like an idiot. He'd already told her he wasn't doing it again, and then he showed up at her door, asked, and she didn't answer.

Maybe she didn't like him nearly as much as he liked her, except... She kept going out with him. She kept saying yes. He assumed she was going to say yes one more time today.

"I thought you said we weren't going to date anymore?" she said, and that was probably the most words she'd put together on any of the dates that they had. Maybe it was because they were in her home, and she felt...safe, he thought with a sudden bit of insight.

"Tomorrow. Tomorrow, I... I can't anymore, and..." He laughed a little. "I guess that's why I'm here tonight. Because this is my last opportunity. I... I just wanted to spend the evening with you."

That was so lame, so lame and so ridiculously dumb. He felt like an idiot, but it was the truth. He was not telling her some half-lie to make her feel better but telling her exactly how he felt. Maybe that's why it was so hard. He felt vulnerable.

"Oh."

He smiled a little. Either Ryland was really out of the loop of the Sweet Water gossip circle, or the gossips hadn't gotten a hold of this. His family was the only ones that he had told, that he would be heading to Rockerton. The courthouse was going to be open for a special session, and maybe that had made the news, but as far as he knew, his name hadn't been linked to it. He thought there were four or five other men who were up for auction.

Still, he just said he wanted to spend the evening with her, and...he wasn't sure what that expression on her face was.

"Could we go to the diner?" she asked, wrinkling her nose.

"We don't have to go anywhere. I...don't want to invite myself in, but I know that there were some shelves in the library that needed to be fixed, and if you want, we could do that?"

Chapter Eleven

Ryland's eyes brightened, and her brows rose way up. "Really? You would fix those shelves?"

"In exchange for food, I'll do pretty much anything," Lucas said, thinking that was a brilliant idea and not sure where exactly it had come from. He certainly hadn't knocked on her door thinking that he was going to do some work in exchange for spending a few hours in her company.

Maybe, maybe if they didn't have the pressure of a date on top of their head, didn't have the unfamiliar atmosphere of a restaurant that neither of them hardly ever went to, and didn't have the idea that they were supposed to be doing things that they weren't, maybe that would make it easier for them to chat.

Of course, he could be wrong. And maybe this wouldn't be any better.

But she already said more than she ever had, and so had he.

"All right. That's a deal. I could make sad eyes chicken? I got the recipe from someone at church, and I believe it came from your family. Would that work?"

He laughed. "That's a great recipe. I love it."

"All right. It won't take long at all. Do you want to eat first or do you want to do the shelves first?"

"Eat." He huffed out a laugh. "Did you think I was going to choose something different?"

"No. But I gotta warn you, I'll be eating my own meal today."

"Oh. You've already decided that if you ever go on any dates again, you're not going to allow your date to buy your meal and then eat it too?"

She laughed. "I get nervous when I'm in unfamiliar places, and I couldn't eat. So no. If we go to a restaurant, you can probably still eat my food. But if I'm with you, the unfamiliar place won't bother me as much, because I'll feel comfortable with you. Does that make sense?"

It made total sense to him. She couldn't handle too many unfamiliar things at one time; she could handle either the man sitting across from her or the restaurant they were in, but being in an unfamiliar place with an unfamiliar person would be too much.

Too bad he had learned that too late.

"We could have gone to the diner before."

"I should have suggested it. I just...didn't."

"It's okay. I think they have better food anyway, although that last steak I had was really good. It's kind of nice that I found a girl who likes steak as much as I do." Though technically he had found her only to lose her.

"I only ordered that because I knew you would be eating it, and I knew you like steak."

"What? You don't like steak?"

She lifted her shoulder. "It's okay. But it's definitely not my favorite. Too much chewing, I think."

"Too much chewing.? I have never heard anyone complain about food for that reason."

"I know. I'm lazy. My mouth gets tired chewing steak."

"Then you've never eaten one that was cooked right."

"Maybe not." She had turned to the kitchen, took a package of chicken breasts out of the refrigerator, and opened it up. "Do I need to do two for you?"

He grinned, and he knew he probably should be embarrassed, but he wasn't. Because of the way she smiled and asked, and she didn't act like it was...a bad thing.

"If you don't mind."

"Two is just as easy as one, and maybe I'll make a third one, just in case."

"All right. Just in case two isn't enough?"

"Yeah. Just in case he's hungry after he puts the shelves together."

He grinned, and it sounded like something his sisters would have said. Which made him smile. And feel like maybe she knew him a little bit, even though she really didn't know much at all. Any more than he knew her. But maybe they could correct that this evening, and then he reminded himself that they really shouldn't. Because he was going to be getting married to someone else tomorrow.

He tried to push that thought out of his brain. There wasn't anything he could do about it, but he also didn't have to sit around and let it ruin his evening, either.

There wasn't anything wrong with just enjoying his evening with her. They could be...friends. He didn't think it was wise for a man to have close women friends when he was married. That was just a recipe for disaster. But for now, neither one of them were, and he wasn't going to think about it anymore.

"What can I do?"

She reached in the fridge and brought out a few ingredients, setting them down and giving him some instructions.

"That's the most you've spoken since I've known you."

"I'm sorry. I...have a tendency to be quiet when I'm nervous. Or thinking. Or, you know, pretty much anytime."

"Except for now."

"Yeah. I guess I'm more comfortable in my home."

"Or the library."

"Yeah, although I'm the librarian, so I feel like I have to maintain a certain standard, you know?"

"Right. An authority figure."

"Yeah. If I let my guard down, people will take over, and there would be a ton of craziness going on, and I won't know how to stop it."

"Makes sense. Give kids an inch, and they take a mile."

"Yeah. Give kids an inch, and they'll destroy the library." They laughed.

"I wish I would have thought of this back when we first started. I... I would like to talk to you."

"I should have suggested it, but...talking. You know."

"Actually, I've often thought that our silences were...helpful to me. Even though they were maybe not exactly the way I would have liked to have our dates go, I did appreciate the fact that I didn't feel pressure to talk. Or to carry on a conversation, or to be funny or witty or know exactly what to say after you said something. I just...felt secure in the silence."

"That's interesting. I sometimes just need silence to process. And I kind of enjoyed watching you. A lot of times, your thoughts show in the expressions in your face."

"I make a lot of hand gestures too," he said, realizing he'd been waving the knife around for a while. He set it down gently. "Like that."

"I was getting ready to duck." She smiled. "I was keeping an eye on that."

She pulled her air fryer out from underneath the counter and set it up, plugging it in.

"Have you seen that dog around again?" he asked.

"That's the reason I need to be home every night at eight. I... I do usually get ready for bed starting at eight o'clock, but I try to feed him on a schedule so that he knows to come to the door before his food freezes."

"You could give him dry food and set it out."

"I know. But I like to mix warm water in it when it's this cold outside. It makes me feel like maybe he's getting something warm in his belly before he goes to bed, and it offsets the fact that he's staying outside in such cold weather."

"Animals are capable of a lot more than what we give them credit for."

"I know. But we have kind of bred them to be the kind of animal that needs us. You know? Most dogs are not bred for the cold and don't have the coat and survival skills to make it through. Cats are a little bit different, but still, this cold weather is tough even on wild animals who are used to it."

"I can't disagree with that. Will he allow you to touch him?"

"No. I haven't even been able to be outside when he's on my stoop. The closest I ever got to him was that night when the boys were chasing him. He came around my back and cowered behind my legs and brushed against me. But I kind of hope that as things get warmer, I'll be able to go outside and I won't feel so bad if I end up chasing him away from the food. It won't freeze, and I can just leave it out there so he can come back some other time and eat."

"That makes sense. That also takes a lot of patience. I think I would probably force the issue," he said as she handed him a wooden spoon and he started to stir.

"I don't really have a lot of choice, and it's a little bit selfish of me, since I don't want to go outside and stand in this freezing cold weather."

"Is there someone who would be concerned about you if you didn't come back in?" he asked, unable to fathom the idea that there was just no one in the world for her. He had eleven siblings, and even though his parents were gone, they would all be concerned about him if they didn't hear from him for a few days. Maybe Lois, who wasn't at the ranch right now, might not be super upset, but he knew he had a group of people who cared about him and would notice if he wasn't around anymore.

"No. I mean, I have an okay relationship with my mom, but...I guess it's just mostly me."

Wow. He knew that she spent a lot of time alone, but he hadn't stopped to think about the fact that she might not have a family, any at all.

"You're an only child?"

"No. I was for the first twelve years of my life. My mom got married that year, and she had a family with her husband. My stepdad is...nice. He is. But, I don't know, I just guess I always noticed that there was a difference in the way he treated me versus the way he treated his 'real' children. Looking back, it makes sense that you treat a baby differently than you treat a teenager, but in my mind, it showed favoritism. They spent more time with the babies, they cooed over the babies, and for me, they were just basically like, did you get your schoolwork done? Here's your chore list, and I want you to watch the kids on Saturday night so we can go out for a date. You know?"

"That's too bad. Maybe they were playing favorites, maybe they weren't, but it's sad that you didn't feel like you belonged."

"Yeah. So, Mom is still in Raleigh with my stepdad and their three kids and their happy suburban family. And I answered an ad that I saw online for a librarian, because this was just perfect for me."

"In other words, you can live at the poverty level and survive."

She laughed, as he had expected, and nodded. "It's true that the pay is not that much. But I guess I don't really need much."

She didn't say anything more, and he supposed it was awkward for anyone to talk about money, although she hadn't shied away from that subject either.

"It's kind of admirable for people to live within their means. And be content with not much. I... I think a lot of times, we do a lot of striving for things we don't need. And things that don't really end up making us happy in the end, you know?"

"I agree. I feel very content here. Sweet Water is an awesome town, and while the winters can be pretty harsh, I love the feeling of being in a snuggly warm house and curling up with a book, some tea, and...I suppose there's something to be said for good company as well."

"Hmmm. I think she might be talking about me."

"You're way too charming. I don't want to give you too many compliments and encourage it, I... I'm not sure what's going on, but I don't like the idea of there not being any kind of future. It seems almost like a waste of time, other than it's fun to get to know someone and chat, and be friends. I just don't know how well male-female friendships work out. Not good ones anyway."

"I suppose that's another thing that we're in agreement on. But I made an exception for you. Just this once. And I decided that I was just going to accept that this wasn't my normal and have a good time. Is that asking too much?"

"No. It just makes me a little bit suspicious, and I feel kind of guarded. Like I should be being very careful, instead of relaxing."

He nodded. He understood what she meant. She didn't want to fall for him, any more than he wanted to fall for her, because there was no future for them.

He kind of wanted to tell her what was going to happen, but there was no point. She couldn't do anything about it, and he couldn't either. Not unless he wanted to back out and pay the fee that would entail, which would ruin the whole point of the auction, which was to solve his family's problems, not create more debt for them.

"I take it from the way you reacted that you don't usually have people coming in and offering to help with shelves and that's a good thing."

"You've seen how long the shelves have been piled there, and no one has offered to help put them up. I actually tried to do it myself a few weeks ago, because I was sick of tripping over them, but I needed two people in order to do the work, and I didn't have the tools to do it anyway. That was according to a couple of videos that I watched online."

"Well, there's two of us now, and I do have tools, though I'll have to go back out in the cold and get them out of the toolbox of my pickup."

"Let's get some chicken in you before you go out, unless they need to warm up before they'll work?"

"I don't think so. It's not that cold out tonight. If it's below zero, they should sit inside for a bit."

The air fryer dinged, and she took the chicken out and flipped it to the other side, putting it back in. "I didn't see you order rice at all, on the last four dates. Do you not like it? I have some instant mashed potatoes."

"I'll take mashed potatoes all day long."

"All right, how about peas to go along with that?"

"Would you believe that peas are my favorite vegetable?"

"Mine too."

Although technically they were a seed, they didn't need to get technical; anything that was green on his plate, his mother called a vegetable and told him it was good for him, and he should eat it.

"Are there any green things that are bad for you? You know, that you should avoid?" he asked as she got the bag of peas out, and he started opening cupboard doors looking for a pan.

"I've never thought of that. Green pretty much means good all the way around, doesn't it? Unless of course you're talking of poison ivy, which I assume would be just as nasty on the inside as it is on the outside."

"I have never eaten poison ivy, so I cannot tell you. I'm sure we could Google and find out."

"Or we can live the rest of our lives not knowing, the way we have the first part."

"I don't feel like I've suffered at all because I haven't known, so maybe it's something we can just think about and not concern ourselves with."

"I think before I ingest any, I'll search it online, but until that point comes. I can't think of anything that is green and causes anything but good things to happen in your body, I guess. Unless of course you're allergic to it."

"Yeah, me either. All the bad things seem to be white or yellowish. Like potato chips. Cake."

"I'm sorry, but the best cake is brown."

"Oh boy. I think we could have a brawl about that. Because no. The best cake is not brown. It is yellow."

"How about a marble cake?" she asked, with one eye closed as she looked at him, before she looked back at the pan and poured more peas in.

"Okay. Marble. Yeah, I think we could do that. That's a compromise, isn't it? I wonder if that's how marble cakes were invented. The couple compromised and had both rather than having them divorce over that argument."

"Well, if you're going to argue about something, cake is definitely worth it."

They laughed together as he grabbed two plates and silverware and set it on the table.

It was funny how he felt so at home in her house. And she was just as funny and her company was as enjoyable as he thought it was going to be.

It made him regret the fact that this was the only time they would have together.

They put the toppings on the chicken and stuck it back in for a few minutes as the peas started to boil. He helped her make the instant mashed potatoes, and it wasn't long before they had supper on the table. An easy, relaxed atmosphere that he enjoyed.

While he loved his house and siblings, mealtime could be chaotic with all the people hanging around. He liked the fact that Ryland was so easygoing, easy to talk to, and he didn't feel like he had to talk nonstop. They could work together in silence, and he felt just as comfortable as he did when they were chatting or laughing.

Regret wanted to bubble up, but he pushed it down. He was not going to think about what wasn't going to happen. He was going to focus on appreciating what had. And he would assume, and trust, that God would work everything out.

Chapter Twelve

"And that's where my family found me two hours later, chatting away, with no idea that the entire family had left, realized I wasn't there, and come back for me."

Ryland laughed and handed the drill to Lucas. He had been telling her the story about how he struck up random conversations with strangers since he was a kid and sometimes got himself into trouble.

He was a good storyteller, and his humor was rather self-effacing, even though he had been a precocious child and probably extremely adorable.

He was humble, and she liked that. His stories weren't necessarily about how wonderful he was, but he emphasized the humor and told them in such an engaging and charming way that she had been totally enthralled. She was shocked when he said, "Hey. It's almost eight o'clock. We probably should go feed your dog. Maybe we can come back and finish these after we're done?"

"We don't have to get them all done tonight, but you're right. I'm glad you remembered. I'd feel terrible if he was out there waiting."

"Maybe I could walk out the front while you go out the back and put the food down, and I can at least try to figure out whether we've got a boy or a girl on our hands? We could name him tonight."

"That's a great idea!" Then she let out a breath. "But it's too cold for you to go outside and stand around."

"I'm from Wyoming, which is not that different from North Dakota. Maybe it doesn't get quite as cold, but our winters are still pretty harsh. I'm tough."

She grinned. She had been having such a great time with him, although the difference between them was stark. She would never have gone up to a stranger and said anything to them. Even now, she had trouble talking to her friends, let alone strangers. Although, she had developed such an easy rapport with Lucas that talking to him was almost second nature.

There was just something about him that put her completely at ease. That, and the fact that they were in the library, where she felt totally at home and completely safe.

Not that she thought restaurants were dangerous, exactly, they were just a new place, and that made her uneasy.

He walked back with her to grab his coat and then said, "I'll go out the front, slip around, and stand still for a while. Just do me a favor and don't lock any doors on me."

"You do me a favor and don't stand outside so long you get frostbite." She was serious, and the smile faded from his face a little as he stared at her. Maybe he realized that she cared about him, or maybe he was trying to figure out why she would be concerned. After all, according to him, this was their last night together.

Part of her thought that maybe he was just telling her that so that she would let him in, but most of her knew that he absolutely would not lie, and that there really was something going on.

He had put his coat on and was zipping it up when she said, "You're not going to die, are you?"

"From the cold? Nah. I've spent hours out in the open, dealing with our cows in much colder temperatures than this, fixing water lines, fence, and looking for animals that were lost. Standing out in the street for a few minutes is not going to be the death of me."

"No. I meant tomorrow. Like, you said tonight was our last night together. You're not going to die tomorrow, are you?"

"I suppose only God knows," he said with a grin, but then she had the feeling that maybe he saw that she was serious or seriously worried. And he sobered immediately.

"No. It's nothing like that. It's...just something that I have to do, even though I don't really want to. You know? You have those things? The things where...you can do one thing, and it will benefit a lot of people, even if it won't benefit you, and you decide that it's a sacrifice worth making." He didn't say anything else, and he just kinda stood there for a moment, then his eyes slid to hers and he seemed to search her face, as though he were wondering if she could understand.

She tried to think of any time she'd done something that didn't benefit her but benefited everyone else. Being a librarian was all about serving others, but she got paid to do it. Even though it wasn't a whole lot, and she had decided to do it because she could afford to. But would she do it if no one paid her? If she starved to death while doing it?

She didn't think so.

"I guess I have to take your word for it. I don't think I've ever been that selfless."

"Sometimes we're just not given the opportunity. I haven't really had too many opportunities in my life to put other people first in a huge way, but when this showed up, I couldn't stand by. It's not the best decision to make for myself, and I know that goes against common, everyday, worldly wisdom." He put "wisdom" in air quotes. "You know, where the world tells us that we should make decisions based solely on what benefits us. I see that all the time, but I couldn't disagree more strongly. I feel like the Bible says the exact opposite. That we should think of others first, and count the cost to ourselves last, or at the very least consider it laying up treasure in heaven when we're doing something that benefits others. Sometimes that looks radical."

"I see," she said, but she really didn't. What in the world could he be doing that would keep him from dating her again, that would benefit a whole lot of people and be detrimental to him?

"Tomorrow will come soon enough. But if you don't mind, I didn't really want to talk about it tonight. I wanted tonight to be...a good memory for me." He grinned. "I've been talking about how I'm doing this big thing to benefit others and I get no benefit, but tonight was to benefit me. It was something I wanted to do that wasn't going to benefit anyone and might be a bad idea... I really, really wanted to see you. And I don't regret a minute. I've had a great time."

"I have too."

His words warmed her heart. She loved that he considered coming to see her something that he was indulging himself with. But she hated the idea that he didn't feel like it was necessarily right or good.

"Just to be clear, tonight has been good for me too. So it wasn't a selfish thing on your part. Not for me."

She didn't want to continue to talk about something that he had specifically asked to not talk about, but she wanted to say that. To let him know that he wasn't as selfish as what he seemed to think he was. That she had benefited too.

"I can't remember the last time I laughed so much." And that was true. She couldn't remember the last time she talked so much either. Especially with a man. She...didn't see too many of those in the library and didn't hardly ever talk to anyone.

He grinned at her. "I'll be outside. I'm not waiting longer than ten or fifteen minutes. I do want to help the dog, at least get him a name, but I don't really want to lose any time with you."

How did he do that? He said things that made her feel...special and like he cared. She felt like maybe she was a lonely old spinster and grasping at anyone who was the slightest bit kind to her, and maybe that was it, but she felt like he really did think she was special.

After all, if he was spending his last night before...before what?

For the life of her, she couldn't figure it out, and she had to admit that she tried pretty hard as she scooped the dog food out and ran some warm water over it.

Taking the pan, she opened the door and called as she usually did, setting it down on the stoop.

She looked around and could see Lucas where he stood at the far corner of the building, against the wall, very still with just his face pointed in her direction, his shoulders parallel to the wall.

She looked around, didn't see the dog, and stepped back in, closing the door.

She shut the lights off and moved the curtain just slightly, waiting to see if the dog would show.

Sure enough, after about three minutes, it slowly walked forward.

The first time she'd seen it, it was a lot more cautious. Now, it wasn't rushing toward the food, but close.

She still couldn't tell if it was male or female, as it came from across the street and she couldn't get a good look.

She couldn't even see if Lucas had slid along the wall.

After a while of standing there, she heard the front door of the library open again, and she hurried out.

"Were you able to see?" she asked as he came through the library.

"We got ourselves a boy," he said with a grin. "Also, I locked the library door, so you don't have to worry about it."

"Thanks," she said, leading him back through the library and into her small apartment. "A boy. So we're looking for a boy's name."

"Yeah. Have you been tossing anything around?"

"No, not really. I guess I was kind of thinking Rosie for a girl, naming him after the lady who started the library in Sweet Water to begin with."

"Rosie. Was that Rosie Stryker?"

"Yes. She actually worked here without pay for a while, and then when the library burned down, she was the one who spearheaded getting donations to rebuild it. There were a few other librarians before I came along, but she still visits pretty often, and I know it's near and dear to her heart. It just seems kind of fitting that if the librarian has a dog, she would be named after Rosie. But that's not going to work."

"Cord's her husband. You could name the dog Cord."

"I guess I could. But I guess that's a little bit weird having a dog who is named after somebody else's husband. Or is it just me?"

"No. I guess I'm glad you don't want somebody's husband hanging out in your apartment."

They laughed a little together as he took his coat off and hung it up on the rack by the door, putting his hat on the hook beside it.

"Are we going back out to finish the shelf?"

"Sure. As long as you're not too tired?"

"Nope. I think you're probably going to have to kick me out to get rid of me." He didn't say anything more about wanting to spend time with her or enjoying it, but the way he smiled at her made her toes curl.

She supposed she should have been embarrassed that she asked him to give her kissing lessons, because it made her sound pathetic and desperate, but she had honestly forgotten about it until just then, and something in the way he smiled made her think of...kissing. Which of course led her to the embarrassing request that she had made of him.

"Well, if we get the rest of the shelves put up, I think we definitely need to celebrate with some hot chocolate or coffee. If that's your thing."

"Any kind of hot drink is welcome on a night like tonight," he said as they walked back out to the library area together.

Not only did he help her put the shelves together, but he also unpacked some of the books that had been sitting around because she hadn't had room for them, and he even helped organize them.

He hadn't been joking about sticking around, since it was eleven thirty when they finally stood back and admired their handiwork.

He had swept up the mess they made on the floor while she finished getting the last of the books on the shelves, and everything looked pristine as they stood shoulder to shoulder, smiling first at the shelves and then at each other.

"I can't tell you how much I appreciate this."

"It's my pleasure, I assure you. I just really appreciate you letting me come in, especially since maybe our time together before this hadn't been exactly the most fun you'd ever had."

"I've enjoyed all the time I spent with you. The silent times, and the times we talked and actually accomplished something. Although, I suppose I would take tonight over the other four nights any time."

"Same. I almost kind of feel like I shouldn't have come, because I was expecting to have a good time, I always have enjoyed being with you, but this... This makes me wish I had more."

Her eyes roved over his face, but she couldn't ask him what he was talking about. If he had wanted to tell her, he would have. And her asking would probably just make it harder for him to not share whatever it was that he didn't want to talk about.

So, instead of asking what she really wanted, she said, "Are you ready for some hot chocolate? Do you have time?"

"I sure do. And considering the time, you better make it coffee."

"All right. Coffee for you, and hot chocolate for me, because if I drink a coffee now, I'll be wide awake until dinnertime tomorrow. Then I'll crash, no matter where I am."

"All right. I wouldn't want you crashing somewhere and endangering yourself."

"You should worry more about the people around me. I feel like I'm more of a danger to them than myself. Somehow, I always manage to escape unscathed, but that's not always true for whoever happens to be in my orbit."

"I like being in your orbit," he said, and he moved over to stand beside her, rather than sitting down at the table. She washed her hands and moved away, grabbing the hot chocolate out of the cupboard and starting the coffee maker.

It felt like there was some kind of tension in the air. Something that she wasn't used to, something that felt a little scary, slightly awkward, but delicious at the same time. Like a romance that was hurtling toward the black moment, and you can see it coming, feel all the fear and excitement that made a reader want to close their eyes, only they couldn't, because obviously they couldn't see the words to keep reading.

"What are you laughing at?"

"Oh. I was just thinking that it's impossible to read with your eyes closed."

He was quiet for just a couple of moments, and then he said, "I think it might be a little late for you."

"Yeah. I told you I start going to bed at eight o'clock."

"Wow. And it's almost four hours past your bedtime. I should be gallant and leave, but I'm going to wait for my coffee."

"I wouldn't let you leave without it. I owe you coffee and more."

"You don't owe me anything. Just hanging out here, laughing with you, was payment enough."

She didn't think that was nearly payment enough, but she didn't argue with him. Instead, she reached up and got two mugs down from the cupboard while he opened the silverware drawer and got two spoons out.

"I should have helped you wash your dishes earlier. I didn't even think about it." He said that before he started running water in the sink.

"You don't have to do the dishes. Guests aren't supposed to come and get put to work right away. And you've been working all evening."

"It hasn't really been work. It's been fun, and maybe I just want to do the dishes to prolong the evening."

"All right. Then I guess if you wash, I'll dry."

It was a deal, and while they waited for their drinks to warm up, they got the supper dishes washed and dried and put away, chatting the whole time.

Finally, with their mugs steaming, they sat down at the table.

"So if you could have anything? What would you want?" Lucas asked, and for once, he seemed serious. He'd been joking and jovial all evening, but the closer the time got for him to leave, the more serious and somber he became.

"You know, I have everything I want. Honestly. I'm happy in the library, I get to read almost as much as I want. I have good friends in the town, and I suppose if we ever name that crazy dog, I wouldn't mind if I could adopt him, but otherwise..."

"You don't want a family?"

She laughed. "I have often thought that I would love to have a family, but that would actually require me to talk to men, or at least talk to one man, and that's not really something I'm good at. As you know."

"You've been just fine tonight."

"I know, but who's going to show up at your door, walk in and start fixing stuff, and make you talk to them?"

He laughed. "Me."

"And you're unavailable," she reminded him softly. She wasn't sure why, or how, or what, but she just knew he wasn't, and she wasn't going to argue or fight it. That just seemed...like it would cause him more stress than what it needed to.

"So, if I were suddenly available..."

She laughed. "There's no point thinking about that though, is there?"

"There's really no point in thinking about the whole subject at all. No one's going to drop in and just grant you any wish you want."

"If someone did, what would be yours?"

"You," he said, and the word was spoken easily. It wasn't said craftily like he was trying to get somewhere with her or like he was embarrassed. It was just a simple statement, like a fact.

She wanted to tell him that he could have her. Although, she questioned whether he really did. They'd spent one evening together. Although, it was a time where they worked together, and he had accidentally pounded her thumb, and they'd gotten through that together. And the second set of shelves they put together incorrectly the first time, and they'd had to take the entire thing apart.

Neither one of them had come unglued just because things didn't work out, and she figured that those were just small tests of their character.

"I guess I wish I wouldn't have asked," she finally said. And meant it. She didn't want to know that. Didn't want to be reminded that what he wanted was what she wanted, and neither one of them could have it, and she didn't know why.

Chapter Thirteen

L ucas drained the last of his coffee. "I probably should leave. It's... almost twelve."

He had been so tempted to bring up the kissing lessons, tempted even to just ask if he could, and he'd been biting his tongue extra hard for the last forty-five minutes. Time had ticked by more quickly than what he wanted it to, but the whole time, he'd been struggling. Wanting to stay, wanting to do things that would prolong his time with her, but knowing he should leave. Should have left a while ago.

"My siblings are going to think I chickened out," he said out loud, and he realized he probably should go.

"They're expecting you to be somewhere tomorrow?" she asked.

He nodded. He appreciated the fact that she hadn't been pushing him to tell her what it was that he had said he couldn't tell her.

Some people when you told them you couldn't tell them something, it just made them want to know so bad that they couldn't think about anything else.

But Ryland had respected his request, and he felt like it meant she respected him. He knew she would be a compassionate listener, but spilling his story to her was only going to make him want to not do it, and he already made up his mind.

He pushed away from the table and stood up, and so did she.

It was five 'til twelve. He had been thinking to himself that if he was going to kiss her, he needed to do it before midnight. Not because either one of them would turn into a pumpkin, but because he didn't want to kiss Ryland on the same day that he married someone else. That would be a little...icky.

He deliberately didn't make any move toward her. He wanted to kiss her, wanted to touch her, to be closer, put his arms around her, and...feel her close to him. But friendship was one thing, and they were already treading on dangerous ground in his opinion, because he definitely felt more than friendship with her. But to move whatever relationship they had from feelings to physical was totally not the right thing to do.

She had stood with him and now faced him, her hand on the back of the chair, as he looked at her, taking a few moments to quiet his thoughts.

"Thanks for letting me in tonight. It could have been...awkward for you, and definitely you had every right in the world to tell me to hit the road, and I appreciate you didn't."

"I'm glad you came. This was the best evening I've had in a really long time. And I'm not just saying that."

"You're saying that being with me is better than reading a book?"

She opened her mouth, let it hang there for a second, and then tilted her head. "I think that's what I'm saying. That's kind of scary. I didn't think there was anything better than reading a book."

He grinned, but inside, he was groaning. After all, to get a librarian to admit that he was better than a book was a pretty big deal.

He took a step closer, even though he knew he shouldn't, and put his hand on her shoulder. "I think you might need to repeat that in order for me to believe it. After all, being that you're a librarian, I assume books are pretty important to you and that they represent a good time."

"Right. They do." And to his surprise, she stepped closer to him and put a hand on his chest.

He wanted to put his hand over hers and press it closer. Wanted to put his arm around her waist and pull her toward him, wanted to lower his head. Surely she could hear his heart beating. It felt like it was thundering, knocking against his ribs and in danger of jumping right out between them.

Her breath seemed shallow, and her fingers curled just a bit.

He moved his so they were cradling hers and squeezed.

"I... I should go. I... I really need to. I... I'll always remember tonight as the best night of my life." He didn't doubt that for one second, and he hated that it had to end this way. That it couldn't end...a little bit differently.

"Same," she said simply.

And he figured that one word said everything he wanted to hear and maybe a few things he shouldn't.

He leaned forward and pressed his lips to her forehead. It wasn't the kind of kiss he wanted to give her, but it was an appropriate kind of kiss. The kind of kiss that he wouldn't be ashamed to look her husband in the eye and say that he gave. And that was probably the best kind, because he would have to look his wife in the eye tomorrow and make vows to her, and he didn't want to have any other kind of kiss hang over his conscience.

"I think I could have loved you," he whispered. Then he turned to the coatrack, shoving his hat on and pushing his arms into his sleeves before putting his hand on the doorknob.

"Same," she said softly behind him.

He didn't turn around. He wished he wouldn't have known that. But he had told her, and maybe, maybe it was a good thing that she had returned the sentiment. He would think about that for the rest of his life as well.

He opened the door and walked out into the cold.

Chapter Fourteen

S he might as well have had a coffee last night at midnight, Ryland thought as she sat at the library desk the next morning around eleven thirty.

She hadn't slept at all, and she didn't want to admit that the majority of the reason was because Lucas walked out, yet again, without kissing her.

Of course, the rest of the reason was that she was trying to figure out what in the world he could possibly be talking about that he had to do that would make it so that they couldn't be together, and he was sacrificing for his family. That he could see her one last time last night.

It just didn't make any sense at all to her, and she couldn't figure it out, and it drove her crazy.

Saturday mornings were typically a pretty busy time for the library, and that morning had been no different. She was actually toying with the idea of keeping the library open past the new twelve o'clock closing time on Saturdays. She wasn't doing anything else the rest of the day, and if folks wanted to come in, she was fine with it. She might as well sit here at her desk and read as sit in her cozy chair and what passed for her living room/dining room/every other room other than her bedroom, bathroom, and kitchen, in her apartment.

She tried one more time to read the book she had open in front of her. It was a good one, one she had been waiting for for a while, although she hated it when authors did this. This author had to draw out the story of this couple for two long series, and finally, she was getting to read their happy ever after, although they spent so much time apart that it made Ryland sad.

But it reminded her of her own life. Maybe, whatever it was that Lucas had to do would only take him away from her for a while. Maybe a decade or two would go by, and they'd end up together to spend the rest of their lives side by side, rather than separated forever.

She wanted to think that, although a decade felt like such a long time.

She didn't want to wait that long. She didn't want to miss out on all of those years, all of that time, all of those shared moments.

But sometimes that's the way the Lord was. They just missed out on things, and they had to be okay with it. Because they couldn't change it.

But that just made her itchy. She needed to know what in the world Lucas could be up to.

She had toyed with the idea of calling Priscilla, who she knew fairly well, from her coming in and out of the library. She had two school-age children, and while they lived in Wyoming most of the time, she had brought them in on occasion. She wasn't sure, but just from her observations, she thought that Priscilla shared custody and didn't get them but a couple weekends a month.

It made her sad, because Priscilla always seemed to have a sadness lurking about her that almost seemed unexplainable. And that could be why. Because she missed her kids.

Ryland couldn't imagine having children and then not spending all the time she could with them.

The thought almost made her decide not to call.

She looked at her phone again. Eleven thirty-two. She had to wait until the library closed. Or at least until the library was supposed to close. She never called or used her phone for personal calls during the time she was supposed to be working.

She didn't have much oversight on her job, but she held herself to a higher standard than that.

Except, what if it was something that...she couldn't even imagine... maybe he was going to Africa for thirty years?

No. That was crazy. What would he be doing going to Africa for thirty years?

What would take him away from her?

Finally, she made an exception to her longtime code of conduct and grabbed her phone, punching in Priscilla's number before she did chicken out. Phone calls weren't exactly something she enjoyed, but this was important, and she was almost breathless when Priscilla answered, "Hello?"

"Hello. Priscilla. I'm so sorry, this is Ryland Solomon calling, and I hate to bother you, but I have a very personal question to ask."

"Okay?" Priscilla said uncertainly. "Does this have to do with my children? Because...I'm already feeling a little fragile, actually a lot fragile, and I'm not sure I can help you," she said, and she almost sounded like she was crying.

"No. This has to do with your brother Lucas, although... Sorry about your children. Is everything okay?" She couldn't stop herself from asking that, because it had just dawned on her that Priscilla was definitely having a hard time, and if she were a good friend, she wasn't going to jump her demanding the information she wanted to know, but rather, she was going to try to take care of whatever issue was going on with Priscilla before she asked for the information she wanted.

"Lucas? Oh. Don't you know?"

It sounded like she was crying, and Ryland wanted to nudge the conversation back to Priscilla and her children, but she also really wanted the information that she needed. "Yeah. Lucas. I saw him last night—"

"That's where he was? With you?"

"Yeah. We put shelves up together in the library for the most part." Ryland hoped she wasn't stepping out of line. Lucas hadn't said that he wanted to keep what they were doing a secret or that he didn't want his family to know. Why wouldn't they know?

They had four dates, and all they did was stare at each other. There wasn't anything going on between them.

Priscilla sniffed. "He wouldn't tell us. Just said he was out. But they left a while ago. A couple hours at least."

"They?"

"Caleb went with him, so he wouldn't have to do it alone. I...think it's a terrible idea, but he's determined to make the sacrifice."

"What sacrifice?" Ryland wanted to reach through the phone and grab a hold of Priscilla, either to hug her, comfort her, because she still sounded like she was sniffling, or to strangle the information about Lucas out of her. What in the world was she talking about? Would someone just tell her already!

"The online auction. Lucas is getting married to the highest bidder."

"What?" She couldn't stop the word from erupting from her mouth, and then she looked up and saw five patrons in the library were all standing at shelves, staring at her. She slid the phone away from her mouth. "I'm sorry. It's an emergency," she said, putting a smile on her face but pulling the phone back up to her mouth immediately, although she toned her voice down. "He's getting married to the highest bidder? What auction? Where?"

"He's headed to the Rockerton courthouse. Actually, he's probably there by now. The auction ends at twelve. And whoever has the highest bid when the auction closes is going to marry him today."

"But it's Saturday." Which had nothing to do with anything other than the courthouse wouldn't be open, and they couldn't get a license. But that was hardly the most important thing. "Where is the auction? Can anyone bid?"

"I'm sorry, it's... How about I just text you the link. It's kind of long."

"Yeah. Sure. Please. Can anyone bid?"

"Yeah. I think so. I mean, it's like any online auction, you have to register. You probably have to put a credit card in, although the high bid was fifty thousand dollars, last time I checked. I don't have a credit card with that kind of limit on it," she said, and through her sniffles and shaky voice, there was a little bit of humor, like she didn't know anyone with a credit card with that kind of limit on it.

Ryland didn't know either, although she did have that kind of money. She had twice that much money, a little bit more maybe, in her savings account. She hadn't gotten around to figuring out how she was going to invest it. She'd looked at it several times, the choices seemed overwhelming, and she ended up doing nothing. The idea of hiring a financial planner or someone to guide her had been on her mind more than once, but she didn't know who or what she should talk to, and again, she'd done nothing.

The link came through, and she clicked on it. As she waited impatiently for the website to load, she said, "Is this an absolute auction? He has to get married?"

"I believe he signed something when he signed up for it. I wish he wouldn't have. The ranch can use the money, and we're going to be in a really bad position without it, but...he's just giving up so much."

That's what he meant. That's why he couldn't get married. That's why he wouldn't kiss her! She stared off into space for a moment. Of course. He might not have known who he was getting married to, but he wouldn't want to kiss her when he was planning on marrying someone else, even if he didn't know who it was. He wanted to be with her. He spent last night with her. He hadn't wanted to leave.

He had told her that he could love her.

She closed her eyes. Then they snapped back open. She still had time!

And then she read right at the top of the web page: "Winner must be present, in person, at the steps of the Rockerton courthouse in Rockerton, North Dakota."

She glanced at the clock. Eleven thirty-eight. It took thirty minutes to get to Rockerton. She would never make it.

Unless...she drove really, really fast. Faster than she'd ever driven in her life before. And left right that second.

Yeah. She could drive fast.

She looked again. The high bid was $52,329. And...if the bid went a lot higher, she might not have enough, with everything she had in her savings account, but...she'd think about it on the way there.

"Thank you so much, Priscilla. I'll call you later, I need to go."

"Okay. Bye," Priscilla said immediately, and she appreciated that she didn't try to keep her on the line.

She stood up, grabbing her phone and her jacket, when she noticed that there were still people in the library.

She'd never, not even one time, left the library when there were still patrons in it. No matter how long they might stay past closing time or how badly she wanted to get away. But there had been several times where she had a headache and closed the library early, and once she'd been sick with the flu and hadn't opened it at all. But she'd never ever left her post. Not while there were still people in the building.

"Bernadine," she called to the lady standing in front of the health and fitness aisle.

"Yes?"

"Please lock up after everyone leaves." She threw the key on the desk, and didn't wait for Bernadine to answer her, but ran out of the library.

She was a terrible driver, absolutely awful. She hated driving in snow, and she hadn't even thought about it, but she didn't even have her car cleared off. There was still snow on it.

She ran out, figuring that it was going to take at least five minutes to get the car so that she could see out of the windshield, but when she went out, it was clear.

There were big prints all around it, and she wondered if perhaps Lucas had cleaned it off last night when he'd been waiting for the dog to show up.

Or after the dog had already shown up.

Regardless, she could figure it out later, thank him for it then too.

She started her car and drove out of town as fast as she could. She could speed on the highway and just hope she didn't get caught.

She never ever did that. To her, the speed limit and all traffic signs were to be obeyed, and it was a matter of character as to whether or not a person obeyed them whenever there wasn't anyone watching. She always came to a complete stop at stop signs. There didn't need to be a policeman sitting nearby in order for her to obey the law, same with speeding. She obeyed the speeding laws, because she shouldn't have to have someone standing over top of her forcing her to do it, but because she was a Christian. Christians obeyed the law because Jesus commanded it.

So, the guilt was heavy on her heart as she went two, then twenty miles an hour over the speed limit.

She inched up to thirty miles an hour over the speed limit and held tight to her car as it began to shimmy and shake.

Maybe twenty-five was her limit. Would that get her there in time? She tried to figure out the mileage in her head, with how fast she was going, and realized that that was pointless. What she really should be doing was figuring out how she could get registered for the auction and bid while driving.

She was going way too fast for her to pick up her phone, but if she had a stoplight on the way to the courthouse, and if it was red, she was going to start registering. She had a plan, and then she said a short prayer, "Lord, if this is Your will, will You help me get there in time, please? Somehow You had me calling Priscilla. Somehow You had me finding out before it was too late. She said anyone can bid. Anyone with the money. Lord, I have the money."

Why hadn't Lucas asked her to bid? Was it because he didn't think she could afford it?

Of course. Of course. He would know how much she made as a librarian. Or at least he would guess. He had even made a comment about it yesterday. She couldn't remember exactly what he said. He asked her if she could have anything, and she had said she was content, and he had implied that she didn't have much.

She wanted to bang her head against the steering wheel, but she wasn't going to slow down enough in order to enable her to do that. Later. Later, she would beat her head against the steering wheel, especially if she didn't make it in time. Because she could. She could bid on him. She could afford him.

Except... Maybe he didn't want her?

No. He had spent his last night as a single person with her. And told her that he thought that he could love her. If she made it there in time, she was absolutely going to bid.

If she had a few extra seconds to spare, she would ask him if he minded, if he wanted her to, if...he could stand to be stuck with her.

They might spend a lot of time staring at each other across the table, with her unable to come up with words, and him... Why couldn't he talk? She should have asked him that yesterday. Did she render him speechless? Maybe he really wouldn't want to get married to her if that's truly what happened to him.

The miles sped by, but it felt like it took forever. The minutes flew faster, and several times, she had her car going so fast she was afraid it was going to shake apart.

She ran over several patches of ice and figured that if she crashed, she wasn't going to make it in time, for one, but also, she supposed she'd rather take a chance of crashing than live for the rest of her life knowing that she could have had Lucas but had been too slow.

The fact that she didn't know him very well and wouldn't have considered marrying him under normal circumstances didn't really cross her mind. Maybe that was something she could think about at some other time, and maybe she would make this decision in haste and then repent at leisure, but she just couldn't let the opportunity go by. Not after last night.

If they hadn't had last night, maybe she wouldn't have been in such a rush. Maybe she would figure that it was just as well. Even though she had some kind of attraction that she couldn't explain, she probably wouldn't have been quite so desperate.

She hit the outer edge of Rockerton at eleven fifty-six.

Her heart was in her throat, and the foot that wasn't on the gas pedal shook as she stopped at the stoplight.

Her hands trembled as she grabbed her phone, starting to fill in her information while keeping an eye on the light. She wanted to get there as quickly as she could, maybe they could stop the bidding until she was able to bid, but no, there was a timer right at the top of the page, and she saw the bid had gone up to $82,000.

That was a lot of money to pay for someone, and who in the world were these people who were bidding on him?

Did he know them?

They had to be at the courthouse steps, that was the rule, so she probably would find out quite soon whether or not she knew them.

Typically, she avoided making a grand entrance, and she tried to blend into the background, because she wasn't the kind of person who enjoyed standing out front and getting all the attention for herself, but in this instance, she didn't even think about that. The only thing she thought was she hoped she wasn't too late.

She parked in the no parking zone, right at the foot of the courthouse steps. She shoved her car in park and popped out of the door, grabbing her phone and typing her address in.

"Ma'am," a male voice said, but she ignored it. "Excuse me, ma'am. You can't park there. That's a no parking zone."

She didn't lift her eyes, didn't respond at all. She had never defied authorities in her life before and wouldn't have done it now, except she only had three minutes to get her info in and make her bid.

No, wait. Two minutes left.

She had trouble getting her fingers to work, and she typed in the wrong address, having to erase the number and retype it.

"Ma'am. Please move your car."

"Just tow it," she said. Knowing that if she bid all of her money, she wouldn't be able to pay the parking ticket or the impound fee to get her car back. But...she wasn't going to worry about that now.

"Ma'am?" The man's tone had changed, like he couldn't believe that she had just said that he should just go ahead and tow her vehicle. That probably wasn't the response that he typically got when he talked to someone about parking in an illegal zone.

"I need to bid," she said desperately.

"Oh. Okay. Here, follow me, and I'll lead you to the steps."

There had been a crowd of people, and she hadn't been able to see everyone, but she didn't need to. She needed to get her bid in. The bid was already high, and she was going to bid every single penny that she had. It was slightly over $120,000, and she wasn't going to be able to move the money today. But surely other people wouldn't be able to do that either. After all, it was Saturday. Surely they were going to have to wait until the banks opened on Monday morning.

"Ma'am?"

"I need to bid first," she said, her words rushed, desperate.

"All right," the man said. "You still have..." He looked at his own phone. "...twelve seconds."

"Twelve seconds?"

She typed in $120,001 and hit submit.

It came back with an error message, telling her she needed to put in a credit card number.

She had never been good with numbers. Words and books and reading was her thing, but she had put in her credit card number so often that she had most of it memorized. Hopefully it was right. Because she didn't have time to get it out of her wallet.

Closing her eyes, trying to picture the card in her head, although she couldn't, she typed in the number she thought it was, adding the expiration date, the code from the back, and her name as it appeared on the card. She typed in her bid and hit submit again.

She wasn't sure whether or not it took her bid because she did not get a confirmation page, all she got was a page that said, *This auction has ended.*

Chapter Fifteen

Lucas stood on the steps of the courthouse beside his brother.

When Caleb had said he was going to come, Lucas had told him he didn't need to bother, but he was really glad that Caleb had not listened to him and come anyway. It was so nice to have moral support beside him.

This was more harrowing than what he had expected.

There were, to his surprise, five different ladies who had shown up on the steps.

Two of them were old enough to be his mother. The other three were probably at least ten years older than he was, if not more. Not that their ages bothered him. He had decided to do this, and it didn't matter what the woman who won him looked like or how old she was.

He just shouldn't have gone to Ryland's last night, because none of them were her, and none of them were even close.

Three of them were pretty bold and brassy, which was to be expected and something that he should have expected but didn't. After all, a woman who was going to bid on a man and was prepared to marry him on the spot was probably not the shy, retiring, wallflower type that he seemed to be insanely attracted to.

If his feelings for Ryland were any indication. She definitely fit the stereotype of the shy, retiring wallflower. And...he loved that he could peel back her layers and see that there was so, so much more to her.

She reminded him of honey and silk and warmth and compassion and... He loved that she was feeding the dog outside her door. She didn't even know whether it was a male or female, and she heated the water before she gave it to him.

That just said so much about her, and he smiled as he thought about it, even as the graveness of the situation descended on him.

The fourth woman looked like she had been recently released from prison. She stood in the twenty-degree weather in a T-shirt, her hair shaved almost as short as a buzz, and her muscles bulging. The muscles emphasized the tattoos she had on both upper arms.

She had big earlobe earrings in her ears, and Lucas figured that if they ever had a fight, a physical fight, she would win, hands down.

The fifth woman needed an interpreter in order to talk to anyone. He couldn't quite place the language, but it sounded like a Slavic language, perhaps Russian.

That woman also looked like she was used to the cold, and he hoped that she hadn't traveled all the way from Siberia just to bid on him and take him back.

He hadn't thought that he might end up leaving the country. He definitely hadn't thought that he might end up living in Siberia.

He tried to take a deep breath. This was not going to be the worst thing that ever happened to him. And he was willingly going through this for his siblings. Because he loved them. Because he would do anything for his family, and by anything, he meant truly anything.

He eyed the woman who looked like she was an ex-con. Yeah. Anything.

He swallowed, trying to shove down the panic that threatened to overwhelm him. It was finally sinking in that what he was doing was for a lifetime.

It had seemed so straightforward and easy when he had thought about it, before he looked at the women, one of whom he was going to pledge the rest of his life to.

He'd always taken marriage vows very seriously. His parents had taught him that divorce should never be an option in his mind.

Whatever happened, he should plan on working it out. However that looked. There would be a lot less divorce if that option was totally taken off the table, except in the one instance where Jesus said it was okay—fornication. Even then, it wasn't something that was necessary, if it was at all possible for the situation to be worked out.

He swallowed. *Lord, I'm scared to death. I'm feeling like this was a huge mistake, but when I decided to do it, it seemed like the right thing. Was I wrong?*

It was a little late to pray that prayer.

He had felt like he was wrong the whole way home last night, when all he wanted to do was stay at Ryland's house and be with her.

There was less than a minute to go, and he shoved his hands in his pockets and tried to look relaxed. Although, he figured at this point that was impossible. He had no idea who was ahead in the bidding, but the woman with the interpreter whispered fervently, gesturing with her hands. Her interpreter looked impassive, like someone off one of those mafia movies, someone who killed people for a living and didn't have a conscience.

That was a terrible thought. He tried to shove it away, but after the woman who looked like she could take him in a wrestling match with one arm tied behind her back, the woman who looked like the mafia guy was her bodyguard would be his second pick of women that he didn't want, which would leave him with one of the women who had the personality that was exactly the opposite of the woman that he...could have fallen in love with.

Which would probably be for the best, because she wouldn't remind him of Ryland at all, but it might be difficult for him to grow fond of his wife in that regard. If she was everything he didn't want.

Still, it didn't matter what she was, he would love her, because love, Biblical love, was a choice and one that he could choose to show on a daily basis.

"Fifteen seconds, bro," Caleb said beside him, and to his surprise, Caleb sounded tense.

Maybe Caleb was having the same feelings he was about the ladies who were bidding.

A car had careened in, but he had barely noticed, because he was focused on which woman he thought he was going to end up with.

There had been a board set up with the countdown, and the crowd now chanted as the seconds ticked under ten, and then they all spoke together, "five, four, three, two, one," and then it was a big letdown because there was absolute, dead silence.

Then, there was some murmuring in the back as a security guard moved, asking people to move aside.

"Excuse me, excuse me," he said as he made a path for the person who followed him.

Lucas figured he shouldn't care who it was, since he had seen the screen, and there'd only been five bidders.

He looked again. Actually, he'd been wrong. There was a sixth bidder. Someone bid at the last moment.

Then, he looked at the winning bid. $120,001. What an odd bid. But it had won.

He swallowed, looking at the board and trying to make some sense of it.

"Ryland Solomon?" Caleb said beside him, sounding like he couldn't believe it. "Isn't that the name of the librarian?" he asked, his voice pitched low, soft, but it squeaked a little at the end, like he couldn't quite believe it.

"It is, except...her salary isn't even that much in five years." He was sure of it. The tiny little bit that Sweet Water could afford to pay their librarian was hardly a living wage. The librarian did the job because she loved it, not because she made money on it. If Ryland had that kind of money, that would have meant she would have had to save every penny for the last five years, and what would she have used to live on? To eat?

"I would agree with you, except...that's kind of an odd name, and that's definitely the name of the person who won."

"Ryland Solomon," the man in charge of facilitating the auction said into his microphone. "Please come to the platform. We will have you sign the contract, and then the judge is waiting in his chambers to perform the nuptials."

The security guard still pushed forward, and Lucas's eyes flew back to him.

None of the ladies that had been standing on the steps bidding had moved when the speaker had said Ryland Solomon.

Unless they were just waiting to see if the crowd would disperse, but...the anticipation was making them press forward, and the security guard was having trouble getting through.

Could it be Ryland? His Ryland?

His fingers had fisted in his pockets, and his fingernails dug into the palms of his hands.

He bit the inside of his cheek and held his breath, trying as hard as he could to get a glimpse of whoever it was that was following the guard. He was a big man, and she was completely hidden behind him.

Ryland. He didn't know any other Rylands, had never heard that name in his life before until she had become the librarian in Sweet Water.

He waited, impatiently, feeling like time slowed to a crawl as the security guard made his way to the front, and he finally moved enough so that Lucas could see the person behind him.

Her eyes met his at the moment he recognized her.

Chapter Sixteen

It was. Ryland. His Ryland. She had bought him.

Lucas couldn't keep from smiling. Couldn't keep the grin that wanted to spread across his face, except she looked scared to death. Her face was white as the snow piled up around them, and her eyes and mouth were pinched tight. She blinked, looking all around, and he remembered that one of her fears, perhaps her greatest one, was standing in front of people with everyone staring at her. And yet, she came.

He couldn't see a smile, couldn't see the happiness on her face, because she wasn't looking at him. Her fingers were clenched tightly in front of her as she kept her eyes on the back of the security guard's head.

He saw her close her eyes for a moment, and her lips moved, as though she were praying.

"This is where you will settle up, ma'am," the security guard said.

"Did I win?" she asked, sounding shocked.

"Your name is Ryland Solomon?"

"It is."

"You won. You're going to have to show your ID and pay, then you're going to the courthouse and get married to the fella. He's standing right there in case you haven't seen him yet."

Her eyes snapped to the man's finger and then bulleted in a straight line to where he pointed. They landed on his face as Lucas felt his heart jump.

Her face didn't exactly break into a huge smile, but the corners of her mouth were definitely tilted up as she looked at him.

"I'll be," Caleb said in an odd voice beside him. "I kind of feel like maybe I always thought God loved all of His children equally, but right now, I'm feeling like He's got a favorite."

"I'm feeling that way too. It's actually a pretty good feeling."

"I bet. Although, for me too, because I've got to let you know, I was feeling pretty nervous about the ex-con down there, and the bodyguard looks like someone who might end up in cement at the bottom of the ocean if he's not careful."

"Or me."

Caleb knew exactly what he was saying, and he laughed and clapped him on the back. "Yeah. That thought crossed my mind too. I thought I might have to kidnap my own brother to get him out of here."

"Really? You'd do that?"

"No. I was just thinking about it. Then I thought about the money, and I decided that that wasn't such a terrible way to die. It'd be quick and painless anyway."

"Thanks. I kind of figured I could depend on you to have my back."

"You know it," he said, but the relief on his face could not be missed.

It probably mirrored the relief on his own.

"All right, I think you don't need me anymore. In fact, more than that, I'm thinking you don't want me anymore," Caleb said, giving him a wink.

"I seriously appreciate you being here." It... It was torture either way, but it was easier having someone, family, beside him.

Caleb grinned, shoved his shoulder into Lucas's, and then said, "I'm going home. I'm going to sit in front of the fire for a really long time. Have a great night."

"You too," Lucas said.

"All right, do you two know each other?" the person standing at the front of the platform holding a clipboard asked as Ryland walked out.

She didn't say anything, and Lucas almost laughed. That was the quintessential Ryland. Not talking.

She did manage to nod, and while the man gave her an odd look, he nodded in return and then looked down at his clipboard.

"All right then, I'll need to see some ID from the lady," he said, clearing his throat and waiting for Ryland to pull out her ID.

She fumbled with a pocket in the inside part of her coat, and then pulled out a small wallet, and then pulled off her glove so she could pull her ID out of the little pocket where it was contained.

It seemed to take forever for her to get her ID out, while the crowd seemed to press ever closer, and the ladies who had been bidding did not move.

A thought crossed Lucas's mind that if Ryland didn't have the money, they might ship him off to the second highest bidder. And at the thought of that, a hard shot of nervousness ripped through him. Surely Ryland had the money. She wouldn't have bid if she couldn't pay, right? He hated to even question it, but he had no idea where she would have gotten that kind of money from, and she seemed a little nervous. But of course, that could be because she hated being in front of a lot of people.

No one had told him that he couldn't walk to her, so he took two steps forward and put a hand on her shoulder as he turned to stand beside her, then he slid his hand around and put it completely around her, pulling her to him.

He didn't know if having him beside her would help, but he did know that having his brother beside him had helped him, so maybe he could be the same kind of sturdy support for her.

It was worth a try anyway, and she didn't push him away. Which was encouraging.

"Thanks," he said, which did not begin to express exactly how he felt, but it was close.

"Why didn't you tell me?" she asked in a low voice, almost a whisper as the man looked at her ID, wrote down her name, wrote a couple more things, and then handed it back to her.

He shook his head and figured they'd have plenty of time to talk later.

"All right. If you can show me your bank account, if you have access to it on your phone, we'll let that work as confirmation for now. I can take numbers and put a hold on it. You'll sign the papers, but we will transfer any funds on Monday when the banks open."

"All right," she said softly as she used her teeth to pull her other glove off, and then her fingers flew over her phone.

She pulled up her account, and Lucas had a glimpse of the amount that was in there before she turned it to show it to the man.

$120,002.

She had bid everything she had for him.

Wow. That was humbling.

Of course, he had made what he felt was a bigger sacrifice for his family, but she had given everything she had to...rescue him? He wasn't sure what the terminology would be, other than buy him, which sounded terrible, but that was what she had done. She had bought him, using everything she had.

She bit her lip and looked up at him, and it looked like she was... sorry.

"I'm sorry," she whispered.

His brows furrowed. Why would she apologize?

"Why?" he couldn't help but ask.

"Maybe there was someone else whom you wanted to win? I didn't get here in time to ask. I...got one bid, and that was it."

That was why she had bid everything she had. It was a good thing, too, since someone had obviously bid one dollar less than she had. But she hadn't wanted to take the chance that she wouldn't get him. Hadn't wanted to lose him. Hadn't played it safe, even though that was her nature.

His chest expanded, and he wasn't sure he was going to be able to contain all the emotions he felt, but he had to reassure her. She had done him a favor, and she didn't even realize how big it was.

He leaned forward, closer, putting his lips down by her ear as his hand went around her waist. He said softly, "Don't look now, but there's a group of five ladies to your right. They're standing there waiting to see if your bid goes through. Those were the five ladies who were bidding on me. And...I will be grateful to you for the rest of my life."

He leaned back, and she looked up at him, her eyes wide.

Then, keeping his hand on her waist, he stood up straight and turned slightly so that they were standing shoulder to shoulder again.

That's when her eyes slid over, and they widened. She took a quick sweep of the group and then another, and then she turned back to him.

"You do owe me, don't you?"

He laughed. It was the sound of relief, of pure joy. God had somehow given him everything he wanted, even though he thought he had been giving up everything. It was crazy the way the Lord had turned things on their head, and in a way that he couldn't even have imagined.

"Everything. Forever," he said, feeling like it probably wasn't a bad thing. He really wanted to get to know Ryland a lot better than what he already did, but he already knew that she was kind and that it would be far better to fall into her hands than anyone else's.

He thought that...maybe the rest of his life was going to be better than he thought it was going to be. They had a lot of things to work out. Like where they were going to live, what they were going to do for a living, whether they were going to be on his ranch, or whether he was going to live in town with her, and he'd drive out to the ranch every day or... He didn't care. He wanted to be with his siblings, sure, and he could see a way clear for that now, but he'd already been convinced that he might have to give it up and he'd been okay with that. He would still be okay with that. If that's what she wanted.

"All right, we can see the money is in your account, and we have placed a hold on that. We will get back with you on Monday to get that transferred. In the meantime..." The man took another sheet of paper that the lady sitting in the chair beside him had been working on filling out. "This is the notarized statement that says that Lucas Clybourn is at your service for the next five years. And that he has agreed to marry you." He picked up another sheet of paper. "And here is the sheet of paper that states that you agree to pay that sum for his services."

The man looked at both of them. "I know that Lucas has already looked over the papers. If you haven't got a chance, go ahead and read those to your heart's content. Once you're satisfied with what they say, we will have you both sign them, have them notarized, and we will file copies at the courthouse on Monday."

He looked between both of them, shifted his hat on top of his head as though he were getting cold, and then he said, "Once that is completed, we'll walk into the courthouse where Judge Roscoe is waiting to marry you."

Of course they wanted to get this over as quickly as possible. There were four other people whose auctions ended today. Once they got out of the way, they would have the folks whose bidding ended at one o'clock up on the podium.

Lucas looked at Ryland. He took the papers from the man and handed them to her. "When you're comfortable with these, we can sign them and get this going."

"All right. Is there anything in there that I should be concerned about?" she asked him, and the trust in her eyes made him feel like he was ten feet tall, but it also made him feel like he didn't deserve it. She truly was trusting him. He hoped he didn't let her down.

"No. I signed them without qualms, and they're fair to you."

They were probably more fair to her than they were to him, but she was the one who had just given up six figures in order to rescue him.

"All right then." She looked at the man. "I'm ready to sign."

She spoke with confidence, but her words were soft and firm. She would never be the brassy, bossy, totally in charge kind of woman that the other ladies on the platform were. She would never be loud and overconfident, either.

And he found that that was just fine with him. In fact, he wanted that. She was soft, but she obviously had a core of steel that he was interested in getting to know.

They signed the papers, and the man said, "Thank you. We'll file these, and we'll send your copy to you in the mail, to the addresses listed on here." He indicated the paper. Then he looked between the two of them and said, "Are you two ready? We can get the marriage taken care of."

Marriage. The word made his stomach drop out from underneath him, but all he had to do was take a glance at the ladies who were gathering up their things and stepping off the podium to make him feel like this was the absolute right thing to do and so very grateful that Ryland had come. He could have been walking into the courthouse with one of them at this very moment, and...if he felt nervous now, he probably would have needed someone to help him walk at that point.

Ryland glanced up at him, and he tightened his hold on her shoulder.

"Are you okay?" he asked.

She smiled a little, as though laughing at herself. "An hour ago, I had no idea this was going to happen. I drove my tail off to get here, and I was so worried that I wasn't going to make it. But I have to admit that the idea of walking in the courthouse right now and saying vows that are going to bind me for the rest of my life... It's scary. Even though... I feel comfortable saying them to you. I just hope you're okay."

She was concerned about him. She had just pledged $120,000 to buy him, and instead of being upset about that or concerned about herself, her welfare, or her future, she was worried about him.

If there was anything that he needed in order to tell him that he was not making a mistake, that was it. And it was perfect.

Chapter Seventeen

Ryland felt a little stunned.

Everything had happened so quickly, and she didn't regret moving fast. If she had been even a few seconds slower, she couldn't even imagine and didn't want to think about how terrible that would have been.

But as they turned toward the courthouse, and Lucas's hand slipped off her shoulder and slid into hers, she felt like she needed a moment to process. Not in a bad way. Just in a way that things had moved so quickly that she didn't feel like she had been able to keep up.

And she needed a little bit of time to acclimate to everything, but instead she followed a man into the bowels of the courthouse where she was about to pledge her life to a man that...she admired, she liked, she thought she could fall in love with, and who had character and integrity and...what was her problem?

She could only hope to get to marry such a man.

She even found herself feeling comfortable with him just last night. And he had come to see her, come knowing that he was going to be marrying someone else the next day, and he wanted to spend his last night of...freedom, so to speak, with her.

Maybe it was the idea that the character and integrity that he had was exactly what she was looking for, if she had ever decided to get married. Or maybe it was the idea that she knew she would be comfortable talking to him, unlike most people she knew, or maybe she knew that he would make her better. Whatever it was, a peace settled onto her. A peace that she'd never felt in her life before, and a feeling that this was exactly what she should be doing, drove out all of her doubts, all of her fears, and she almost felt like she was walking on air.

They stopped for the clerk and got their IDs out, and while the clerk was looking at them and filling out some paperwork, Lucas leaned down to her. "You look happy."

"Is that right?" She looked up at him, and she knew her face was glowing. She really was happy.

"Yeah. I... This is your wedding day, and I hate that it's not better for you."

"It's perfect." She meant that. She had never been someone who wanted a great big production made out of her or anything, although it was perfectly okay for those people who enjoyed that. But that wasn't her. She wasn't a big show kind of person. She wasn't a big crowd kind of person. She wasn't even a little crowd kind of person.

"I don't understand how you can look so...happy and peaceful."

It was like Lucas could see but couldn't understand the glow that seemed to start in her heart and flow out of every pore of her body.

"I have a man of character and integrity. I've dreamed about that, and I'm not afraid to talk to you, which is a little bit crazy, because that's not something that comes naturally for me. But more than that..." She shrugged her shoulders. "More than that, I just feel peace. God has totally taken away all of my doubt and fear, and I know that this is the absolute right decision."

"All right, if Lucas Clybourn and Ryland Solomon will step forward, we'll begin," the judge intoned from where he stood behind a small counter.

It wasn't the way Ryland had pictured her wedding—although she had never dreamed about anything large, she always thought it was going to be a preacher and not a judge—but it worked. She said vows, so did Lucas, and while there were no rings, when they left there was a piece of paper that said the state viewed them as married.

"That was fast and easy," Lucas said as they stepped out into the bright sunlight of a cold February day.

"Yeah. I hadn't realized that that was all there was to it. Anybody can do it," she said.

"I think that's why some states have waiting periods. It's way too easy to just wake up one morning and decide to go to the courthouse."

"That's not exactly how it happened, I... I ran away from the library in order to come. I've never done that."

"I owe you far more than thanks, but thank you. I... I never dreamed that this was going to work out the way it has."

"I have no idea what's going to happen now, but...did you drive?"

"No, my brother Caleb brought me. I'll need a ride home with you if that's okay? I can drive."

"It's fine. I've got it," she said as her brain turned.

She might be married, but she didn't think she was quite ready to actually act married. She just needed to be alone to process things for a bit and try to figure out where exactly she wanted to go from this point.

And then she realized, from now on, it wasn't going to be just her making those decisions. They had to make them together. She had to consult someone else before she could do something as simple as figuring out what she was going to do with the rest of her day.

Well, probably they ought to talk about that, and talking wasn't exactly her forte, so maybe that was something else she was going to have to get good at.

She waited until both of them were in the car, and she had gone through the stoplight at Rockerton and was back on the road toward Sweet Water before she spoke. Uncharacteristically, Lucas had been quiet too, and she wondered what in the world he thought of all this.

Maybe they would talk about it at some point, but she felt like maybe she should get something straight and they should figure out what was going to happen the rest of the day before they discussed it.

"So, I guess we gotta talk about what we're doing."

"You're in charge." His words were subdued, although his eyes twinkled a bit when he looked at her.

"No. That's not how this is going to be," she said, shaking her head even as she looked back at the road. "No. I know what the paper said, but you can forget those. I'm not going to be in charge. It's not you being my slave or whatever the paper said."

"Basically I do whatever you want me to for the next five years."

"Is that what you want? Is that what you think this should be?" She wasn't thinking that in any way, shape, or form. That wasn't what she had in mind at all.

"It's what I agreed to."

"All right. That's not what I want."

"What do you want?"

He had derailed her with those words. She was thinking this was a traditional marriage. Where the man was the head, and she submitted. A Christian marriage where they lived out the Christian principles and guidelines that God gave in His word. As the woman, she would be the keeper at home, he would be the provider. Maybe she would work, and maybe he would help with the children, but they each had their roles, the places that God had ordained for them to be, and they could figure out whatever worked, understanding that God knew best.

But that wasn't what he was saying, and she didn't know how to argue. She didn't know how to present her case, or maybe she knew what she wanted in her mind, she just couldn't get the words to come out of her mouth.

They drove in silence for a while, with her thoughts all jumbled in her head, and no words formed for her to try to share what was in her mind.

She did know one thing she wanted. But she wasn't even sure whether she was going to be able to say that much.

As they got to Sweet Water, she drove through town and past the library.

"Where we going?" Lucas asked as she made no move to turn in and park.

"I'm going to drop you off at your ranch," she said, trying to infuse some determination in her voice.

"Why?" he said, and then he said, "I guess I do need to pick up some clothes. I had packed a few things, but I never thought to get it out of the truck and Caleb drove away with them. Good thinking on your part."

"No. I'm dropping you off there."

"What?" he said, sounding as though his entire thought process had stopped.

She could see out of the corner of her eye that he studied her with a thoughtful look. She kept her hands on the wheel and her eyes straight ahead.

"We're married. Are you going to live at the ranch?"

"No. I'm going to stay at the library where I've always been. I'm going to drop you off at the ranch."

"So... We're going to pretend this never happened?" He paused. "Do you want your money back?"

"No. I don't know how things are going to go, because that money was in my plan. But I don't regret spending every cent of it. You had said something last night about making a sacrifice to save your siblings. I assume that the reason that you put yourself up for auction was because you needed money for something for them. That's yours. You don't have to tell me about it—"

"We needed it for the ranch. I don't recall if we talked about it or not, but in order for the ranch to stay solvent until this summer when we can start making money on some of the things that we started, feeders and weaners and horses, we need that money to pay our bills."

"And it's yours. I'm not talking about the money."

"But we're married. You're talking about that, right?"

"Yes. We're married. And...that means something to me. But I don't think we're ready to be married. So I'm going to drop you off at the ranch."

"Okay. I get it. You're gonna drop me off at the ranch, and I'm going to stay there and you're going to...?"

"I'm going to go back to the library. I'm going to do what I usually do."

"And what about us?"

"I need to think about that. I don't want it to be where I tell you what to do and you're like my slave or something. That's not what I want."

"But it's what you signed up for."

"But if I say that I want something different, then you have to do that, right?"

"I guess."

"But I don't even want that. I don't want to be the one in charge calling the shots. That's not me."

"All right. What do you want?" he asked as she slowed down and pulled in behind a car at the main farmhouse. She had no idea whether that was where he lived or not. From what she understood, there were several houses on the property, although she never had a tour of the place. She'd been there once or twice to visit Alaska and Priscilla, but she never discussed Lucas while she was there.

"I want kissing lessons."

Chapter Eighteen

So he was going to be teaching her to kiss after all.

Lucas shook his head as he got out of the car and slammed the door. He watched as Ryland drove away.

Maybe he should be upset. He got married. His siblings had thrown a going away party for him just this morning, and now here it was, not even two o'clock the same afternoon, and he was back. It was like he had never left, only now, he was married. And that meant something to him. But there was also the fact that he had signed papers that stated that he was under Ryland's authority, and she could tell him what to do for the next five years.

That had taken some of the luster off the marriage, when he realized that it wasn't going to be a real marriage. It was Ryland in charge.

But when he tried to make sure that she understood that he was going to live up to what he promised, she balked. He didn't understand.

But the lessons he could get on board with. Before he got out of the car, she said that they could continue their Monday dates, and they could include kissing lessons. But maybe instead of going to Rockerton, they'd just go to the Sweet Water diner.

He had been fine with that. More than fine with that. Especially with the kissing lessons. He supposed he should tell her that he really wasn't qualified to give lessons in that area. But if that's what she wanted, that's what he would do.

He'd been so caught up in thinking that he hadn't realized that his siblings had filed out of the house and were now standing on the porch as he had watched Ryland drive away.

He turned around, and they were staring at him.

"She doesn't want you?" Rufus asked.

Rufus was the youngest brother and third from the end.

In Lucas's opinion, at least right then, he was also the most foolish.

"As long as she didn't want the money back," Caleb quipped.

"No. She made sure to tell me that the money was mine. But it's more than what we need."

"Then maybe you should give that back to her," Ezra said, his arm around Alaska and baby Alice in his other arm.

"Maybe." He had thought about that, that they could offer to split the money. The idea was she would be in charge, calling the shots, but the money was his.

He supposed that if she didn't want to be in charge, which is what he thought she was saying, then he would give her half the money. Maybe he should just give it all back to her. He wanted to be with her anyway. Although, marriage wasn't exactly something that he would have done at this moment in time in their relationship. But it was done, and he didn't want to undo it.

"So why did she let you off here?" Asher asked, his voice a little hesitant, like he figured that was probably a touchy question, but it was the question on everyone's mind.

Asher stood with his arm around his wife, and Lucas felt a minute of jealousy. After all, he now had a wife, but...he couldn't say she didn't want him. Because she did. She asked for kissing lessons, but she dropped him off and, under no uncertain terms, wanted him to stay at the ranch. At least, that's what he thought.

"I guess everything happened pretty fast this morning, and we're married. The judge signed the papers." He stopped. His words were just getting all tripped up over themselves. He took a breath, tried to gather his thoughts, and started again. "But I don't know where we're at with everything else. I don't think she did either. She...just found out about the auction this morning."

"She called me and asked what was going on. I hope it's okay that I told her. I mean, the auction was public knowledge."

"So you talked to her?" Lucas asked Priscilla.

Priscilla nodded. "Didn't she tell you?"

"She didn't have a chance. She showed up with like twelve seconds left in the auction, bid on me, signed the papers, we got married, and she dropped me off here. We...didn't really talk about anything." He really wanted to talk to her. He knew that talking wasn't her thing, but... sometimes people had to do things they weren't comfortable with.

"Maybe she dropped you off to get your truck?" Asher suggested.

"Maybe." He supposed he could drive in and see her. That's what he wanted to do. But she had specifically said something about Monday dates.

"She wants me to date her on Monday."

"She doesn't want to talk to you again until then?" Ada asked, and she sounded like she didn't believe that for one second.

"I don't know."

"I'm sure she wants you to see her. She might've said that she needed time, and maybe you should give her an hour or so, but she wants you. I promise you that," Claudia said, and he didn't doubt it. Claudia was more outspoken and maybe the most opposite personality from Ryland, but he supposed there were characteristics that defined females in general, and he assumed she thought that was one.

"What makes you say that?" he asked, coming to the bottom of the steps and putting one foot on the second step up while he put a hand on the banister.

It was cold out, but warmer than it had been, which made it feel balmy and pleasant, accelerated by the sunshine, which was melting some snow despite the cool air temperature.

"Because women like to know their man wants them. And one of the ways that women know that is by having her man chase her. Not literally, I don't think she wants you running around the house after her—"

"Although she might," Alaska interrupted to say, and the entire group laughed.

"Noted," Lucas said dryly. He had a hard time imagining Ryland running while he chased her, but he had a picture in his mind of her jogging around the library and the shelves, and him ducking around looking for her, and her laughing, and him finally catching her, and... Yeah, he could get into that.

"Women really like to be chased?" he said, feeling like an idiot with his entire family standing there staring at him and him possibly asking questions that maybe he shouldn't be. He didn't want them to know more about his private life than what they needed to.

"They do," Sondra said with confidence.

"I would agree with that," Phoebe said. Which meant something to Lucas, because Phoebe didn't always have a lot to say.

She was typically rather quiet, and when she did talk, he definitely wanted to listen.

Because she often had wisdom that came from having thought about things more deeply than other people. Kind of like Ryland.

"Why don't you just ask her?" Priscilla said, and that seemed like a really good suggestion. He appreciated it, especially since Priscilla was struggling with demons of her own. He had been kind of wrapped up in his own affairs and also in the financial issues of the ranch, but he thought that maybe Priscilla was going to end up moving back to Wyoming. She had been struggling all winter to be away from her children, and it had been very difficult for her. Her ex was not making things easy, and if she moved back, she might have more of an opportunity to...if not get full custody, then at least see her kids on a more regular basis.

He wasn't sure of all the details, and Priscilla hadn't shared them. She just had seemed very unhappy a lot of the winter, and he thought that perhaps she'd been crying a good bit too.

He wished he could help her, but helping the ranch become financially stable would be a good step in that direction anyway. She wouldn't feel like she needed to stay. Maybe she would be more free to pack up and leave, especially if she had some money behind her.

"I guess I should."

"Maybe you should give her a little bit of time. This morning was kind of chaotic. She basically screeched into the courthouse and bought you. It was a pretty large sum of money, and if she just talked to Priscilla this morning and found out about it, she couldn't have had much time to make that decision. But maybe you could chase her a little this evening." Caleb's smile was slow. Lucas didn't have any trouble reading exactly what his brother was thinking when he said the word "chase," although Lucas wasn't sure that was exactly what his sisters had in mind.

"I think that's a good idea. Give her a little bit of time, and then go see her this evening. So she knows you're thinking about her and that you want her. She might doubt that." Tobias spoke, and his words were slow, thoughtful, and Lucas stopped everything to listen. "But I'd expect to sleep here tonight if I were you."

With that, Tobias lifted his hand from the railing and then said, "I've got work to do. Congratulations on your marriage."

He clapped Lucas on the shoulder as he walked by, and Lucas smacked him on the back as he descended the steps.

That broke the party up, and his siblings dispersed as he walked back in the house. When he had left this morning, he wasn't sure whether he would ever be back. He certainly didn't expect to be back later that same day.

Just went to show how small his vision was compared to the vision that God had for his life.

Now, if he could just keep from messing everything up. Because one thing he was sure of, when he had told Ryland last night that he could fall in love with her, he might've been a little slow with his assessment. Because he thought he already had.

Chapter Nineteen

As Ryland parked her car and got out, she realized Grover - the name she'd decided to give the stray dog - was waiting for her by the back door where she usually fed him.

It was so odd that the dog was around in broad daylight and not running as she got closer.

In fact, Grover whined.

"Hey there, buddy, what's going on?" she asked, glad to have something to take her mind off the events of the morning. It had been a whirlwind day, with so many things happening that she wasn't even sure what exactly was going on anymore.

Except, she was married.

Married to Lucas Clybourn, with whom she had one amazing date and four dates that...were very forgettable. Just for the fact that they hadn't said anything at all.

"Hey there, buddy," she said again as she got closer and the dog didn't move.

In fact, he got up and put his nose against her door, whining some more as his tail slowly moved back and forth.

"Grover. What's going on with you?"

He just whined again and put a paw up on the door, scratching gently.

"You want in?" That was so strange, since up until that point, she hadn't even been able to get close to him except for that one time the boys had chased him.

"Are you tired of being cold? I think you and the rest of the population of North Dakota are ready for spring. I know I am."

Grover whined again as Ryland opened her door. She didn't always lock this door, and she definitely hadn't thought to lock it as she had raced out of her house just a couple of hours ago, having no idea that her life would change so drastically before she walked back in.

"Let me get you some water. Maybe you're having a hard time finding a place to get a drink. Everything's frozen, isn't it?"

She always put water in the dog's food, but maybe she should be more careful to make sure that the dog had some fresh drinking water every day as well.

She hadn't even really thought about that. Of course he could eat snow, but she knew, for humans anyway, it was impossible to stay hydrated and warm when a person had to use their body heat to melt enough water to drink.

"I'm sorry I wasn't more considerate," she said to Grover, who walked in the mudroom door and whined some more.

His behavior was so odd that Ryland took a moment to really look at the dog. So mangy and matted and skinny, despite the fact that she knew he had been getting a good meal every day for the last few months, since she had first seen him.

"I need to go in and check the library. I ran out really fast, but here, here's my old coat. You can lie down on it if you want to, then I'll be back out." She threw her coat down, then, at the last second, decided to fill up a little container of water for the dog as well. She'd come back out and do more for him, but she did need to check the library and make sure that Bernadine had locked everything up the way she had requested as she had run out.

Maybe she'd even give Bernadine a call.

She set the pan of water on the floor, and Grover watched with deep, intelligent eyes until she had stood up and backed away from it, then he moved closer and took a drink. She touched his head softly, but his lapping did not stop. Not wanting to press her luck, she took her hand away, smiling.

He was still drinking as Ryland slipped through the door, intending to check things out and run right back.

She stopped in her tracks as she saw that Bernadine sat at her kitchen table, her hands folded around a steaming teacup, her eyes on Ryland.

"And where have you been, miss?" Bernadine said, looking over her glasses that sat on the tip of her nose and giving Ryland a look that a mother might give a teenager who had just slipped in at two o'clock in the morning.

"I... I had an emergency." She knew that the news of her marriage would be all over town if it wasn't already, but for some reason, she felt a little protective of the knowledge, like she just wanted to hold it to herself for a little bit, at least until she had figured out how to deal with it and processed it on her own.

This wasn't exactly the kind of thing that a person could do and then immediately accept as settled. It took some adjustment. Going from a single woman, one who expected that they may indeed remain single for the rest of their life, to a woman who was married to a man who could actually be the man of her dreams. And it all seemed like a big accident, except she knew that God's hand was in everything. It always was, and maybe she just had a little bit of trouble accepting the fact that God was being so good to her.

"I hope you don't think that explanation is going to satisfy me," Bernadine said with her brows raised.

Ryland had never snuck in after curfew. She had never even stayed out until her curfew. She didn't even know she had a curfew. It wasn't necessary. She certainly had no desire to go ramming around in the middle of the night doing she didn't know what. What did teenagers do in the middle of the night? She had no desire to do anything but read books; she didn't even stay up chatting with her girlfriends on the phone. She wasn't a chatterer.

There were a few times when she might have gotten up early, at three or four o'clock in the morning, and gone out somewhere to watch the sunrise, but her parents had never said anything about it. Her mom had never complained, and her stepdad didn't care.

"Do you mind if I get some tea first?" she said, hedging. She really didn't want to sit and have a heart-to-heart right now, but maybe it would help her process what exactly had happened in her life.

"Go right ahead. I can wait," Bernadine said, like she had all day.

She probably did. She was retired.

Of course, what else did Ryland have to do? Even though she was married now, her husband had hopped out of the car, and...he didn't exactly look happy to be free, but he didn't beg her to take him back to her house with him either.

She kind of wished he would have. She felt a little bit like he didn't want her, even though he'd done exactly what she asked him to. That was the thing about being a woman. Sometimes the things that she wanted people to do weren't the things that she *said* she wanted them to do. Which was a bit of a mystery to herself as well as to the rest of the world.

She wanted him to...want her. After all, she was the one who had raced to get to him in time. She was the one who paid six figures for the privilege of marrying him. He hadn't even told her what was happening. Hadn't mentioned it at all to her, hadn't asked her if there was any possible way that she might be able to be the one, because he wanted her.

It had been all her chasing him. She wanted...just a little sign from him that he wanted her. That it wasn't just her doing all the chasing and all the wanting and all the sacrificing. That despite the fact that there was a contract between them and he was required to be with her, that he would choose to be with her even without that contract.

She didn't know how he would show that, how he could even start, but it was what she wanted. She wanted to know that he didn't need to have someone with a sledgehammer over top of his head forcing him to spend time with her. That he wanted to do it because he liked her and wanted her for herself.

That he would have married her, despite the money.

But she knew that wasn't true. He would have married whoever was the top bidder. He had thanked her for bidding, thanked her for buying him, and indicated he thought she was the best out of the six of them, but...he would have married anyone.

And that... That was done.

Even though she admired his sacrifice, admired what he was doing for his family, and knew that he wasn't doing it because he wanted to, but because he loved his siblings.

Maybe she just wanted to see if there was something there for her. Something that he could give to show that he would sacrifice that much for her.

"If you don't mind, I'm just going to take a walk around the library while my water is getting warm, just checking things out."

"I locked up like you asked me to," Bernadine said casually.

"Thank you. I really appreciate it," she said, opening the door between her apartment and the library and stepping into the cool darkness.

Bernadine had even turned the heat down. She closed the door behind her and leaned against it, closing her eyes and sighing. It felt like she was home, and the familiarity surrounding her gave her peace.

Lord, what a day. Did I do the right thing?

And then she laughed. What a terrible time to ask that question.

"You let me get there in time. You let me submit the winning bid. I guess I didn't even think about the money. It... It seems silly for me to keep it in my account for myself when someone else actually needs it right this minute. That doesn't really bother me at all, although...it changes things a bit for me, because it's going to be a lot tighter to try to live here on my librarian salary."

She didn't have any housing expenses, and her car was paid for. But eventually that car would wear out, and she would need a new one. What was she going to do? And then she remembered that she wasn't supposed to worry about the future. She was only supposed to live in today and walk in faith.

Of course, she kept forgetting, but she had a husband now. These problems weren't going to be just hers, they would be his as well, and she knew Lucas would take care of her.

Lord, I've always depended on You to take care of me, because there's never been anybody else. But now You've given me someone I can depend on. Thank you. I... I guess I don't know for sure whether he'll really feel like it's his job to take care of me, but the idea that there is someone who cares, someone who will care, is so nice. So very nice.

She leaned her head against the door and just let that thought sink in. That she wasn't alone, that there was someone beside her now. Even if he wasn't with her that second, she knew he meant those vows that he said and knew that despite the contract they'd signed, he wasn't going to walk away from her in five years. He wouldn't walk away from her ever, because he was the kind of man who would keep his vows.

But every man was subject to temptation. Any man could fall. The Bible was clear, take heed, lest you fall.

Women too. Women could fall.

Lord, I don't want to succumb to temptation, especially in my marriage. Lord, keep my eyes on You and help me to do right, please keep my marriage strong and make it last until we die.

Marriage was supposed to be a picture of the union between Christ and the church. It was supposed to be a glorious picture, beautiful and heavenly.

She wanted that for her marriage, but...she didn't really have a whole lot of ideas of how to go about it, and she'd just kicked her husband out at his farm and told him to...give her kissing lessons.

She didn't even know if she could talk to him again. The idea made her nervous, but the idea of kissing lessons? That was even worse.

Lord, help me be brave.

It felt like being brave to talk to him. To face him again after what she'd done. She practically set a record between Sweet Water and Rockerton, in order to get to him. He would have to know how much she cared.

Was that such a big deal? Maybe it was a good thing.

She pushed away from the door. She had company, and she needed to get back to the rest of her life. She couldn't spend it all thinking; as much as she might enjoy rolling ideas around her head and trying to figure things out, she had to actually live her life. Not just think about it.

She went and checked the door, walked around the library as she always did when she locked up, and saw everything was in its place.

Bernadine had done a good job.

Taking a breath, she put her hand on the door and walked back into the kitchen.

Bernadine sat exactly where she'd left her.

So, Ryland made her tea, took it to the table, and sat down.

"So, spill." Bernadine didn't say anything else.

"Lucas was up for auction. He was selling himself in order to raise money for the ranch, to get them through the winter, until they could start seeing money from their various investments. I—"

"He was selling himself?"

"Yes. As a husband to the highest bidder. I found out from Priscilla this morning. And, I guess... I guess I wanted to go and bid on him. Because we had dated some." That was maybe a little bit of an overstatement, but she stuck to it. "And I liked him a lot. He had hinted that there was something going on, but he didn't tell me what."

She still hadn't quite figured out why he hadn't. Did he think that she wouldn't be able to afford him? That seemed reasonable considering her librarian salary wasn't a secret, and there weren't a whole lot of people who knew about her inheritance.

That was a question she wanted to ask him.

"Why didn't he?" Bernadine probed.

"I'm assuming it's because he didn't think I could afford him. The bid when I first saw it was above $50,000."

"Well. That's highbrow stuff."

"It takes a lot of money to run a ranch." She said that like she knew what she was talking about, but she really didn't. She was just assuming. She'd never actually priced a tractor, but...she couldn't imagine that it was not several times more expensive than a car.

"I suppose it does." Bernadine's eyes blinked fast, like she was processing that information, and then she speared Ryland with another penetrating gaze. "Where is he?"

"I dropped him off at his house. We had to sign a bunch of contracts and all that, and he brought clothes, but he forgot to get them out of Caleb's truck in all of the excitement."

"I suppose it would be a little disconcerting, selling yourself to the highest bidder. It seems very...low class."

"Yeah. I guess it might, but I suppose when you need money, it's better to get it however you can, and to be able to pay your bills, than to sit around and consider yourself too good to stoop to whatever it takes in order to make ends meet."

She was defending him. She didn't even know why he had done it, he hadn't even talked to her about it, and still she was defending him.

But he was her husband. Of course she would defend him. To the death, she would defend him, because...that was what a wife did. That was loyalty. That was faithfulness. That was on her. That was character on her part. It had nothing to do with Lucas or anything that he did.

As his wife, it was her job to stand beside him, to support him, to defend him if he needed it, and to be loyal, to help him. However she could in whatever way she could. That was her job, her duty, what God had given her as a wife to do. She hadn't realized she felt so strongly about it, but Bernadine's comment had brought out all of those things. She hadn't even considered that that was the way she should, and did, feel.

"My goodness. You're a little touchy."

"He's my husband." It was that simple. She couldn't talk badly about him, because if they were one, talking badly about her husband meant she was talking badly about herself, correct?

"This seems very...unbelievable. But..." Bernadine paused, her finger tapping on her coffee cup before she drained the last of it.

She stood. "But I believe you. And if this is true, I admire both of you. And that is the honest-to-goodness truth." She nodded her head. "All right. I'll leave you alone for the rest of this Saturday afternoon. I suppose as a newlywed, you want your privacy. If you need someone to man the library for you for a day or two, or if you guys are going away on a honeymoon and you need someone to fill in, just let me know. It's...a dream job. You're blessed to have it."

"Thank you," she said, managing to get words out of her mouth even though she was rather shocked at the crazy way that conversation had gone.

She stood too, although she'd barely taken more than a sip of her tea, since it was too hot, and followed Bernadine to the door where she grabbed her coat off the rack.

She had her hand on the knob when there was a knock at the door.

Ryland hadn't gotten her call to come in out of her mouth before Bernadine opened the door and stepped back.

"Well, if it isn't the happy husband, coming home." She looked back over her shoulder at Ryland. "This one's a keeper." And then she looked back at Lucas. "You have a wife who is one in a million. Make sure you take care of her." With that, she slipped through the door, walking carefully because there were slick spots on the sidewalk.

Chapter Twenty

Lucas glanced at Ryland, and then he looked back at Bernadine, blinked for a minute, and then looked back at Ryland. "What was that all about? Although, I do agree with her."

Ryland laughed. "Want to come on in? It's been a crazy day, and the activity hasn't ceased at all."

"So I'm welcome to come in?" he asked as he stepped inside and closed the door behind him.

"Of course. You're my husband."

"I don't know, you kinda kicked me to the curb at the ranch."

"I'm sorry. I... I guess I just feel like you didn't have a choice about marrying me. I didn't want to feel like we had to do anything that married couples do, including being together, if that's not what you want."

"I signed a paper—"

"I know what you signed," she said, putting her hand up to stop him. "And that's what I'm saying. That's not a marriage. You doing what you have to do because you signed the paper. I want you to do it because you want to, not because there's some kind of paper hanging over your head that says that you're going to. And I know, I know you're the kind of man that keeps your word. I wouldn't have married

133

you otherwise. But I don't want you to just keep your word because you have to."

"I see. You want to know that...I have feelings in the game."

She laughed. "Yeah. Feelings rather than skin. That's good."

"I told you last night I did. That was why I was here. I thought you knew that."

"Why didn't you tell me what was going on last night?"

"I didn't think you'd be able to afford me. I didn't want to make you feel bad. I didn't want to...make you feel pity or whatever it is. I just wanted to be with you, and I thought I knew that that was all I would ever get."

"I wondered. I thought maybe you thought I couldn't afford you, and you would have been right, except my aunt gave me an inheritance a while back, and it's what enabled me to move out of my parents' house, and quit my job in the HR department of a large corporation, and move out here, and have my dream job as a librarian."

"I didn't think anyone could actually live on that salary."

"I pretty much do. I haven't touched much of my inheritance. If I want to do anything beyond eating and sleeping and driving to the grocery store, I have to. So I mostly just stay home and read, and I'm happy with that. Although I've used it to buy health insurance."

"I see. I guess maybe...I wanted to talk about what we want to do. I don't know if you want to wait until Monday, but that's okay if so. I really just wanted to see you."

"Thanks. I really appreciate that, because I know me just dropping you off kind of made it seem like I didn't want to see you, but I wanted to see you because you wanted to see me, not because you had to. So... thanks."

"Can I stay?"

"Of course. You can...do whatever you want to. If I could rip up that paper, I would. To me, this should be a marriage like a regular marriage. Not me in charge. Because that's not what a marriage is supposed to be."

He nodded, seriously considering what she was saying. "I should give you your money back then."

"Technically I haven't paid you yet." The money wasn't going to transfer until Monday. "But no. We've already talked about the money. You put yourself up for auction for a reason, and you told me that your siblings need it. I don't."

"You might. At some time. I don't want you to regret just giving it to me and not get anything in return."

"Well, I did get a husband in return, but I want a real husband, not someone who feels like he has to be here because he signed the paper." She stood for a moment, her hands gripping the back of the chair, as she thought about it. "Can we destroy those contracts?"

"We probably can. Do you want to...get our marriage annulled?"

"No. Not the marriage. I made vows, those vows were before God, so no. I have no intention of breaking those. It's the contracts for the money and for your service for five years."

"I suppose. They were being filed by the courthouse, but if both of us want to destroy them, we probably can. That's just my guess."

"Then let's do that."

"So..."

"So I will transfer the money to you. That's a given."

"No. That was the point. If we're going to destroy papers, the money is yours."

She wanted to fight. She wanted to stomp her foot in frustration.

Instead, she pressed her lips together and looked down at her hands. How was she going to handle this? How could she get him to see that as long as those papers were between them, she couldn't be sure that what he was doing was for her and not because of the papers? And that the money didn't mean anything. She wanted him to have it.

Just then, a noise from the mudroom made her look at the door, and she stared at it for a good three seconds before she remembered. "Grover!" She started toward the door, then she turned and looked at Lucas. "I forgot to tell you. When I got here, Grover was standing in front of the mudroom door. I walked in, and he walked in with me!" she said as she walked over, intending to open the door. "It was so weird. I mean, he even let me pet him."

"He might have some kind of...rabies or something."

"Is that what rabies does?"

"I've heard it makes animals act differently than what they normally do. But also, it can make them attack you for no provocation."

"He seemed fine. Not really interested in having me touch him, but he really wanted in. He stood at the door and whined. I opened it, and he walked in. I put my old coat down so he'd have a place to lie down, and I gave him some water, but I was going to come back out and feed him."

"All right. Let's do that. Although, he might not be house-trained."

"Yeah. I didn't even think about that. I just thought he was too dirty for me to let inside, and I kind of thought about giving him a bath, but since I've never even touched him before, I thought that might be too much."

She opened the door and stepped out into the mudroom, then she squinted.

Grover lay on her coat, but was there something else moving on her coat too?

As Lucas stepped into the room, he flipped the switch by the door, and the lights came on, illuminating everything in their incandescent glow and chasing away the shadows that lay beside Grover.

"I thought you said Grover was a boy?" Ryland said, confusion heavy in her tone.

"He is."

"No. He's not." She turned, putting her hand on her waist, looking at her husband. "I think that you and I might need to have a little chat. About boys, and girls, and their differences."

"Very funny. I know it was a boy. I saw—" He broke off, because he apparently saw the puppy wiggling beside her. Him. No. Her. "I think you might be right."

"Yeah. I think I might be. Maybe you need to get used to saying that," she said, hoping she was able to tease him.

He laughed. And that gave her a sense of relief. He wasn't going to be upset with her if she picked on him.

"All right. That's not hard to say. If you're right, I hope I can give you credit for it."

"Thanks for letting me pick on you. But definitely, we need to come up with a different name for our dog."

"Oh? We have a dog?"

They stood and looked at each other, both of them grinning. She didn't know what was going through his mind, but hers was...that this made it feel real. The marriage, everything, if they had a dog. It was real.

"I guess I shouldn't get a dog without consulting with you first."

"I suppose it's probably a good idea for us to talk about decisions like that." He looked over at the dog in the corner, formerly known as Grover, soon to have a name change, and then looked back at her. "Especially when she's pregnant."

"Yes. Except... Someone told me that she was a boy, and since boys don't have babies, I wasn't too concerned about the idea that I was going to be adopting more than one dog."

"So, how many did she have?"

They both turned back, and walked a little closer, but didn't get too close. They didn't want to scare her.

"I think I see three."

"I'm glad she came in. The puppies probably would have been okay today, but it's going to get so cold this coming week that...they might have frozen."

"Yeah. She...seems to be a pretty smart dog."

"Yeah."

"What about Grace?" she asked after they'd looked at her for a little bit more.

"You mean as a name for the dog? Or as a theme for our relationship, since I think it's only by the grace of God that I'm married to you right now and not someone else. That was...a foolish thing for me to do, but God worked my foolishness out for good."

"For me."

"For me too."

"And Grace?"

"That's a good name. It does seem to be a theme in my life lately anyway."

"Perhaps in mine too. I... Sometimes I can be a little stubborn and, okay, maybe a lot stubborn and suspicious."

"Oh. Is that what that is? You want me to chase you for a little bit because you're suspicious of my motives?"

"Is it terrible that I want you to chase me? I mean, I didn't tell you that, but somehow you figured it out."

"I have sisters." He looked like he was about to say more, but then he closed his mouth.

She wondered if his sisters had told him or if he had observed them.

"They told me that you might want that. After all, it's kind of like you said, no one wants to have someone forced on them, who's with them only because they have to be. Normally you'd see that I have a choice, and that I choose you. But you can't see that, so you want me to pursue you. And just for the record, I'm more than willing to do that, because I do. Want you, that is."

She smiled. "All right. I guess I thought that the marriage was kinda sudden and maybe things are moving too fast. Can we...go back to dating? Just for a little bit?"

"Whoa. Does that mean you don't want kissing lessons?"

"No. I definitely want kissing lessons. And now, you have an excuse, but," the smile faded from her face as she said seriously, "I just didn't want you kissing me because you had to. That's...revolting."

"Yeah." He took a breath. "I was thinking about that while I was standing on the steps, looking at the women who were bidding on me. I was thinking marriage, I was thinking... You know, taking out the trash, providing for the wife, I wasn't thinking...kissing. Until I was standing there looking at them and realizing that I didn't want to kiss any of them. Only you."

"You would have done what you had to do."

"I don't know. I guess I won't have to know now. God intervened, and He sent me a race car driver, who arrived in the nick of time to sweep me away."

" I did drive kinda fast. I didn't realize my car could go that fast."

He laughed. "I don't think I want to know how fast."

"No. And honestly, after I got above ninety, the car started to shake so bad that I couldn't take my eyes off the road to look to see how fast I was going. I would just slow back down until it stopped shaking."

"Okay. I do not want to hear this." He put his hands over his ears, like he was going to drown her out.

"No, really. That's probably going to be one of my favorite stories, after I stop being all...crazy surprised that I'm married now."

"We have a fun marriage story to tell our children—" He broke off at the end of children, and then his eyes widened. "If we have children?"

"I have to learn to kiss first. I... I think that's the first step, right?"

"Was your mom one of those moms that told you that you could get pregnant by holding a guy's hand?"

"No. My mom was the kind of mom who really didn't care what I did. Especially after she met the man she's married to now and kinda forgot about me."

"Well, her loss is my gain. I'm glad you moved to North Dakota, I'm glad you became a librarian, and I'm really glad that your aunt died, God rest her soul."

She laughed. He was being irreverent, but it was funny. "I didn't know her very well. But I think she felt bad for me being with my mom, and you know. Lots of kids have that happen to them though."

"I guess. Doesn't change the fact that it stinks."

Chapter Twenty-One

Tobias Clybourn used the drill to put yet another screw in the porch. It was almost finished, and it would be safe for Mrs. Wells to go in and out of.

She hadn't asked him to do it, but he had seen for a while that it needed to be done. After he'd given Ezra the money that he needed in order for Ezra to be able to get custody of Alaska's children, Tobias had intended to build a house for himself and use the remaining money that he had saved, but instead, he'd walked by Mrs. Wells's porch, seeing that it needed to be fixed, and realized that there were several other people in the area, not just in the town of Sweet Water, who could use his money more than he could.

So, he'd been staying in the cabin at the edge of the property—it was small but suitable for his needs—and instead of building himself a house, he'd been spending his money on fixing up things for other people.

Mrs. Wells being one of them.

The door opened, and Mrs. Wells's cane thumped on the new floor.

She used an arm to hold the door open while she took slow steps, walking out the door and over to where he knelt on the porch.

She held a coffee mug that steamed in the cold afternoon air.

"I thought you might need something to get yourself warmed up, son," she said as she handed him the mug.

"Thank you, ma'am," he said, taking the cup from her and blowing a little before he took a swig and found it was exactly the temperature he liked. Hot enough to burn his tongue.

"This is good," he said.

"You looked like a man who liked it strong and black and hot."

"You judged me correctly, Mrs. Wells."

She nodded, then said, "I didn't think I was gonna ever walk out on this porch again. You made it look good as new. I already told you I couldn't pay you, and you said it was okay, but I feel bad nonetheless."

"Well, don't feel bad. It was my pleasure."

"I'm not used to getting things I don't pay for."

"That's really not the way life works, but in this instance, it was an exception to the rule."

"Sometimes exceptions are good, but you are an exception who works." She nodded her head at him and then looked out at the sky before she said, "Feels like we're going to get some snow later."

"I'll trust you on that one. My body is just saying it's almost time for bed."

"Your back must hurt. You need a wife to go home to so she can put some of that back lotion stuff on it and rub it in real good. I used to do that to my man when he'd come in. He'd lie down in bed, and I'd rub his back until he fell asleep."

"Sounds like you were a good wife. He was a blessed man."

"I think I was the one who was blessed, except God took him too soon. I've been a widow for almost twenty years, and it's been lonely."

Her voice had faded off like she didn't typically complain about anything that was wrong with her life.

In his experience, most of the older folks that he knew, especially the ones that still lived out of town, on the ranches that they'd farmed all of their lives, didn't complain. They just got up every morning and did what needed to be done.

She sighed, then said, "If you're hungry when you're finished, I got some leftovers heated up in the oven. It's going to be dark soon. You can eat before you go."

"Thanks, Mrs. Wells, but I've got some chores to do at home. I better not stay."

"I figured," she said, then without saying anything more, she turned around and shuffled back into the house.

She had gotten dressed up in big, bulky clothes, and he assumed that the cold probably really bothered her, and it was a sacrifice for her to come out in it. But he appreciated it. Because the coffee went down good and warmed him from the inside out.

He drained the last of it and set the mug on the banister. He just had another ten minutes' worth of work to do before he would be done with the entire porch, and he figured he might as well get at it. Picking up a board that he'd already cut to fit, he adjusted it and grabbed a screw from the container.

He liked what Mrs. Wells said about a wife, but that wasn't going to happen for him. Not now, not ever, most likely. After what happened to him back in Wyoming, he wasn't going to go down that road again. He...knew falling in love was a foolish decision. One that could lead a man into doing things that he would regret for the rest of his life. Particularly if he got emotionally entangled with a woman who wasn't right for him.

Or who decided she wanted someone else. Maybe because her family didn't approve of the man she wanted.

And she wasn't going to resist them.

Although, if Tobias had a choice, he would have chosen the girl he thought he loved and put his faith aside, but that really wasn't a choice. He couldn't live without God, and though he found it hard to live without the woman he wanted, he couldn't find it in himself to regret his choice. He just regretted...pretty much everything else.

He sighed, picking up the board and picking up another screw and drilling it down. They were so busy in the summer that he often didn't have time to go around and help anyone, so while winter was not the ideal time to be building anything in North Dakota, he did what he could.

And while he didn't relish going home to his cabin and being alone, he didn't particularly mind. He'd gotten used to it, he supposed. And he was one of the blessed ones that had a family that he could turn to, visit when he wanted to, and then retreat from when the laughter and the noise got to be too much.

Not everyone had those choices. Take this Mrs. Wells for instance, who didn't seem to have any other family. She didn't really have a choice except for to be alone.

He could ease her loneliness some this evening, but he'd declined her invitation.

Maybe he shouldn't have. It wasn't necessarily something he wanted to do, but that didn't mean that it wasn't the right thing to do.

As he finished up and gathered his things, putting his saw and drill in the pickup and taking the extra wood and putting it in her woodshed, something that might be useful for a project down the road, he started to head back to his pickup and then...changed his mind. And the direction of his steps, as he turned around and headed toward her back door.

He'd go on in and sit down with her for a while. He wasn't going to be putting her out, he would probably be doing her a favor, and maybe it would help heal his heart in some small way.

Chapter Twenty-Two

Sunday night, Lucas stood at Ryland's door, waiting for her to open it after he had knocked.

He almost hadn't made it to church that morning. Everything had been frozen solid, and the tractor hadn't started, and chores had taken three times as long as they normally did. Normally he didn't need a reason to go to church, but knowing that he'd see Ryland probably helped him work harder and longer and get things done in order to make it. But they'd had a pile of work to do when they got back home.

So, here he was, six o'clock, after dark, but wanting to spend more time with her. He...missed her. He went through his day, constantly thinking about what she would be doing. His fingers might have been frozen, his feet feeling like blocks of ice, and his entire face burning from the wind, and all he could think of was Ryland and what she was doing. Whether she was thinking of him.

He had almost pulled his phone out and messaged her several different times. Even though it meant taking his gloves off and exposing them to the cold, he didn't care. He just wanted to...talk to her.

He knew they were still together, knew that they were still planning on making sure that their marriage worked, but he supposed that was why married people stayed together, lived together, did things together, because when they were apart from someone, it was harder to keep the doubts and loneliness at bay.

"Lucas! It's freezing outside. Come on in." Ryland opened the door and stood back. He walked in quickly, and she shut the door immediately. When it was this cold out, a person didn't want that kind of air inside the house.

"This was a terrible day to be outside. I hope everything got fixed quickly."

"Not really. We just got done for the day. I didn't even shower." He should have. Looking back on it, he knew he should have cleaned up first, but he knew she liked to go to bed early, and he figured he could leave and shower after he got to see her.

"My goodness. I'm sorry. You can use my shower if you want."

"I never thought about that. I didn't bring any clothes."

"Oh," she said. Then, she moved toward the kitchen. "Did you eat anything?"

"I had some coffee and some chili around lunchtime, but I haven't had anything since, and I'm starving. That's one thing about working in the cold. It really builds an appetite."

"I'm sure. Probably takes a lot of calories to stay warm."

"I guess," he said, hanging up his coat and hat and walking in. She was his wife, but they greeted each other like they were just friends. He wanted to put his arms around her, hold her close, feel her warmth, know that she was real. He couldn't imagine what would have happened if she hadn't bid on him, but he didn't even want to go there again. He knew he wouldn't feel like this with any of the other women and marveled again at the way the Lord worked things out. Now if he just didn't flub it up. He didn't know how he could do that, or maybe more accurately, he didn't know how he couldn't.

"Ryland?"

"Yeah?" she said as she scooped what looked like a hearty beef stew into a bowl.

"I...missed you." He wanted to ask if he could hug her. But he just couldn't quite get those words to form on his tongue, they sounded weird to him.

How did he ask someone if he could hug them? It was such an odd request. But he supposed maybe he should be willing to make a fool out of himself for his wife.

"Ryland?"

"Yeah?" she said as she pushed numbers on the microwave and started it.

"I wanted to hug you."

"Wanted to?" she asked, her brows furrowing as she turned fully toward him and looked at him for the first time.

"Want to. Now. May I?"

He felt...humble. Scared a little, like she might turn him down, hoping she wouldn't. She had every right to. He didn't have any more rights than anyone else, even though he was her husband. She hadn't really granted him any special privileges. Other than the title of husband, which he supposed came with an assumption in most cases, but not theirs.

She tilted her head, as though she were trying to figure out if he meant what she thought he did, and then she shook her head, but she moved forward, throwing her arms out and not stopping until her front was pressed to his and her arms wrapped around him.

"Of course. I'm sorry. I'm just such an idiot," she said as she squeezed him tight. "I never even thought that I should do a little more when I see you other than say hi. You're...my husband."

"I just don't feel very much like a husband right now."

"I think that will change. Right?"

"Yeah. I think so, and it doesn't have to change overnight right now, I just... I miss you. I wanted to call you several times today."

"You could have."

"Really? I wasn't sure whether I'd be bothering you if I called you as many times as what I wanted to."

"No. Truth be told, I almost called you. I had my phone out to text you several times, but I knew that you were working, and it was probably going to be a pain in the butt for you to drag your phone out of your pocket just so I can say hi to you."

"So, maybe I should get something straight right now and tell you that you can call me anytime. You can text me anytime. From now and for the next seventy or eighty or a hundred years, however long we live, I will always welcome hearing from you. Always. It will never be an imposition."

"Even if I just text you hi a hundred times a day?" she asked, her nose wrinkling up as she leaned back a little, keeping her arms around his shoulders and trying to look into his eyes.

"Yeah. Just because it's from you, I'll read it and smile. I like that connection. I know that it may not be the thing that you need, but it definitely is something I need."

"I get it. You need the words. I need the actions. I need to see that I mean something, and you need to hear it."

"Yes. I guess that's true. Although, I'll not turn down seeing it either."

"All right. I'll keep that in mind."

"This makes me feel a little bit more like a husband," he murmured as he rested his head on top of hers and breathed in her scent. It was... perfect.

Exactly what he wanted to come home to after working outside all day, and being able to still do what he loved, and not having had to give it up after all. It was amazing that God had given everything back to him that he thought he was going to lose and added even more to it. He supposed God had said that when a person gives, God will give even more. He had just experienced that in his life and couldn't believe how generous God was.

"I suppose it makes me feel more like a wife as well. At least the fact that you're here. That definitely makes the atmosphere of my whole apartment feel completely different. Better," she added as the microwave beeped.

He squeezed her for just a second more before he let her go. She walked over, taking it out and stirring it up before sticking it back in for another minute.

He supposed she should set the table or something, but as soon as she pressed start on the microwave, she walked back and resumed her position in his arms.

"Now, that's the way a wife is supposed to behave," he said, grinning, because he knew his sisters would give him a hard time saying something like that. Like there was some way that they were supposed to behave.

"Really? So you're training me?" Ryland said, and he laughed. He had expected her to at the very least poke him back, but she did something a little sideways as to what he expected, and he liked that. He liked that she was just a little different, that there was another dimension in his life that hadn't been there before. It just made him feel better.

"I suppose. Although I think it's more likely that you'll train me. Speaking of training, how is...Grace?" He almost said Grover but remembered the sex change just in time.

"She's been doing good. I thought she might be a little protective of her puppies, but she actually allowed me to go over and pet her on the head today. I left her outside for a little bit, and she seemed to naturally want to go out to do her business. At least, she hasn't made any messes inside yet. Thankfully. Aside from my coat, which I'm afraid might be ruined."

"Oh, that reminds me. I totally forgot, I had thrown a dog bed that we had sitting around in the house in the back of my truck. I thought we could use it for her."

"That was really thoughtful of you."

"Hang on a second, I'll go out to get it."

He didn't bother to put his hat or coat on, since he was just running out to his pickup and grabbing it out of the back seat.

Ryland didn't say anything to admonish him to be more careful. He almost expected her to. But maybe that would come in time, or maybe it was just the kind of woman she was. That she was going to allow him to make his own decisions and wasn't going to try to micromanage him.

He kind of hoped that she didn't, although he didn't mind being told what to do, as long as she didn't do it in a bossy way. He kind of felt like her concern for him meant she cared.

He supposed there would be times where he couldn't listen to her, and he wondered if that would upset her. It was kind of hard for him to picture Ryland getting mad, but he knew that more than one man had been surprised when his sweet, kind, darling wife threw a temper tantrum.

He hoped he did not join those ranks anytime soon.

As he walked back in, closing the door behind him and rubbing his hands together and stomping the snow off his boots and on the mat beside the door, he said, "Do you ever lose your temper?"

She laughed as she looked up from where she had set his stew on the table. "What in the world made you ask that? Did you do something?"

"No. I was just thinking I couldn't really picture you angry, but then I figured that was the way most men were until they saw the girl that they had fallen in love with throw a temper tantrum. I just want to know if I was going to enjoy that type of display."

"Enjoy?" She laughed.

He held up the dog bed. "Should we take this out to Grace?"

"Sure," she said, walking the few steps to the door and opening it.

"I have noted that you did not answer me, by the way."

"All right. I guess I'd like to say no, but I suppose that there are a few things that make me angry. But probably it won't surprise you if I say, when I get angry, I have a tendency to get really quiet."

"Oh. One of the many benefits of marrying a woman who doesn't talk much. I think I can really get into this."

"Although, maybe I can take a few notes from your book and throw temper tantrums the way you do it."

That made him laugh. "Well, you probably don't want to do that, because I might say a few words that you'd rather not hear."

"Really?" And she chuckled. "I guess we all have our things. I don't typically have too much trouble with that, but I do have the problem that when I get angry, it takes me a really, really long time to get over it."

"But it takes a really long time to get angry in the first place?" he guessed.

"Yeah."

"You sound like Tobias. I think I can count on one hand the number of times he's gotten angry in his life, counting from childhood. But the few times that he's gotten angry, it's been epic."

"Yeah." She gave a self-conscious laugh. "Epic is probably a good word to describe me when I'm angry."

"So, in the next fifty years, I'm going to see that...four times?"

"Maybe," she said, nodding as they shuffled things around and made room for the dog bed on the floor. "That sounds about right, I guess. Maybe a few more. Once every five years?"

"Boy, I don't know if I can handle that. Although, I probably get angry once a week, maybe twice on a bad week, although it probably depends on how good my wife is to me. If she's a real sweetheart, maybe once a month."

"Well, I guess you can't count on that then." She laughed as she put her hands on her hips. "Do you think we should attempt to pick up the pups and put them in the bed?"

"I don't know. If we just let it sit here, will she move them on her own?"

"I think a cat might, although I think cats put their kittens at the exact spot that you really don't want them. In other words, if you set a bed down for your cat, she's going to put her kittens anywhere but the bed."

"Yeah. That's like forty percent of the reason why I'm not a cat person."

"Oh, you're not? I didn't see that in the fine print of the contract that I signed. That would have been a game changer."

"Funny, since I would have guessed you're not a cat person either. At least you didn't have one."

"I used to. I did for a while when I was younger, but then we moved to an apartment where we weren't allowed to have animals, and I had to give it away. I cried for a week. Mom actually didn't even make me go to school after the teacher called the first day and asked if she could come get me because I was disturbing the class with my sobbing."

"That bad?"

"Yeah. Mom actually spanked me because I had been bad in school. And I suppose in a way, she was right. It was one of those if you don't quit crying, I'm going to give you something to cry about kind of things?"

"I see. That's kind of weird though, since you don't seem like the kind of person who ever did anything to draw attention to yourself. I would have guessed that you would have quit crying if you were able to."

"Yeah. That was the issue. Part of my sobbing was made louder because I tried to not sob, which just makes the sound that you actually make even worse."

"I think I might have to take your word on that, but okay."

"You have six sisters. You mean you don't know this?"

"Uh, no?"

"Wow. Either I'm really weird, or your sisters are one of a kind."

"Maybe both?"

"Are you serious? Don't make me throw that beef stew in the garbage can."

"And here I thought I was making a noble sacrifice by getting a bed for the dog before I eat, even though I'm dying of hunger and am probably about to expire of starvation in any moment."

"It was really nice of you to make sure that Grace had a bed first. How about we go eat that beef stew, and we'll check later to see if she moved the puppies, or maybe we will get brave and do it ourselves."

"Yeah. I'll have to think about how badly I want to be bitten by a dog today. And then we'll see."

"I've been thinking about that all day too, and I just decided that that's not what I want with my life yet."

"We're in agreement on something else. Neither one of us wants the dog to bite us today."

"It's uncanny the things that we agree on."

They went in, both of them smiling. It was easy to laugh with her, to joke with her, and to talk about serious things with her too. After those first four terrible dates, they'd found their groove.

Chapter Twenty-Three

They set the table, and he said a short prayer thanking God for the food, and he added a thankful statement about his life as well. He really felt like he could spend the rest of his life thanking God for what He had done the day before, and it still wouldn't be enough. Talk about epic.

As he started to eat, he said, "So did you ever get your cat back? Or find out what happened to it? Get another one?"

"Oh! I forgot the bread," she said, hurrying to the oven as the buzzer went off and pulling out a loaf of freshly baked bread.

"That was perfect timing," he said with a little bit of disbelief in his voice. It had been a long time since he had homemade bread.

"Yeah, I figured that I was going to be alone tonight, and it just seemed like a good night for some homemade bread and butter."

"I think the butter is the part of that I really like."

"I like them both equally and both a lot."

She walked to the refrigerator, got a stick of butter out, and set it on the table before she went back to cut the bread.

He thought he might have to ask her about the cat again, but she started talking as he put another spoonful of stew in his mouth.

"I went back to the shelter every day just to see her. They got kinda tired of seeing me around, I think, but the owner had compassion on me, probably because she was a cat lover too, and she offered me a job cleaning cages. I mean, she didn't pay me anything, but that allowed me to get Musketeer out and cuddle her for a little bit while I cleaned her cage."

"She seems like a nice lady."

"She was." She sighed and then brought a plate and a piece of bread over, which she set down in front of him. "They never did find anyone to adopt Musketeer, and we moved away while she was still in the shelter. I... I cried again when we left."

"That's sad."

"Yeah. At first, it was just across town, from a small house to an apartment that didn't allow pets, but we moved a lot, and the next move was to a different town in a different state, where Mom had found a job that would pay a little bit more than the job that she had."

"That's tough. I've only ever lived in two places, our ranch in Wyoming and our ranch here. I can't imagine bouncing all over the place and especially not having my brothers and sisters to bounce along with me."

"Yeah. I guess maybe Musketeer kept me company a little bit, but then I didn't have her, and even though when Mom got married, she said I could have a cat again, I didn't. I just... It was too hard to lose her, and I didn't want to go through that again. I guess that's silly."

"I don't know that I agree with that, but I think a lot of people feel that way. I've heard people say that they didn't want to get married again, or they didn't want to have that kind of emotion in their life, because it was so hard when you lost it. But I guess to have it to begin with is part of what makes life worth living. You know?"

"I suppose you would know because of losing your parents."

"Yeah. It's not like I'm confused about whether or not I want more parents." He laughed a little, but it wasn't really something that he found overly funny. So his laughter lacked a lot of humor. "But I definitely would do it all again if I could. Even though that was probably the most painful thing I'd ever gone through. Maybe just losing one wouldn't have been as painful. You know?"

"Or one could have just gotten hurt and been in the hospital for a long time. And you had to take care of them, that would be difficult as well."

"It would have been painful, too."

"It would have been...hard to watch them suffer on a daily basis, plus, living without their spouse would have been difficult as well. I guess if I had to choose, I'd rather lose them both."

"I guess I wish I would have known that I was going to lose them in the first place. I might've done things differently. I mean, I suppose it was a good lesson, because at any point, you can lose anyone, you don't have any warning, you don't get to say your last words, you don't get to say the things that you wish you would have said. You don't get a do-over. You only get to look back and see how you could have done so much more, said the things that you should have said, told them how much you love them, how much they meant to you, and then acted that out, by...whatever it is. I just have so many things I wish I could go back and redo, and I try not to think about it because you can't change it. It's done. It's over with. And you don't get to fix it. But the lesson is there."

"That's a really great lesson. I suppose of all the lessons that you could learn in life, that would be probably one of the best. To cherish each moment that you have, and make sure that you don't leave words unsaid." She laughed as she sat down, setting a plate in front of her with bread on it slathered with golden yellow butter. "It is a good lesson for me. I have a tendency to not say the things I should. Just because my mouth never works like I want it to."

"Really? I hadn't noticed."

She paused for a moment and then huffed out a laugh when she realized that he was being silly. "So those four days where I said absolutely nothing the entire date weren't a dead giveaway?" She shook her head with her lips pressed together. "And he married me anyway. That's probably the shocking thing."

"Oh. And I thought the shocking thing was I took you out on the date, bought your meal, and then ate it myself, and you married me anyway. That to me is the shocking thing."

"I guess that just shows that we can be surprised by different things."

He finished his bowl of stew and looked around, still hungry.

He had taken a breath, getting ready to ask her if he could have some more, when she said, "Want another bowl?"

"You read my mind. I really like it when you do that."

"Well, when it comes to food, it's pretty easy. That's one thing I learned on those four dates, where I might not talk a whole lot, but I figured out that when it came to food, too much is never enough."

He laughed as she stood up, taking his bowl and going back over to the container where she had the scoop, and dipped out some more for him.

"That was really good, by the way. I guess I should have said so, but I suppose talking to you always makes me think about stuff, and I wasn't really paying attention. But if I had to choose between the stew and the bread, it would be a pretty hard toss-up."

"It's the bread hands down for me," she said airily as she put his bowl in the microwave.

"So, if I hadn't come tonight, what were you going to be doing?"

She chuckled and then turned, putting a hip on the counter.

"Never mind. Let me guess."

"Okay. Guess."

"You were going to check on the dog, and then get a good book, and read."

"Bingo," she said, laughing with not a little bit of irony. "I'm so hard to figure out."

"Well, maybe if we made it a little bit more challenging the next time, I'd have to guess the title of the book you are going to read."

"Now that's a good idea. I hadn't considered that. So what would I read?"

"I think I might need a little bit of time to get to know you. And with that thought, when I came here today, I wasn't actually hoping for a free meal, although...that was definitely a nice perk. Although, I'll take the hug any day."

"Really? Hug over food? I'm not sure I believe that."

"Believe it. Because it's true. Maybe next time, I'll have to turn down your food, just to prove that the hug was the whole reason I came."

"Yeah, I think that's a see it to believe it."

He laughed, thinking that she probably was going to make him put his money where his mouth was, so to speak. "Anyway, I was hoping we could read together."

"I don't think you read any of the books that you checked out for the last six months."

"I was here because I wanted to see you. Checking out books just seemed to be what everybody else was doing, so peer pressure. What can I say."

"I don't think I have ever heard that before. 'I checked out books because of peer pressure.'"

"Have you ever heard, 'I checked out books because the librarian was so compelling and attractive that I would do anything to be in her presence'?"

"Nope. Haven't heard that one either."

"Well, now you have. Because that's the truth."

"Wow. I wondered why you were in here checking out books. That just was something I could not figure out, because I knew you couldn't possibly be reading those crazy titles. I didn't understand why anybody would even write a book called *Toe Fungus - a pictorial tome*."

"Hey. That was actually pretty good."

She looked at him for a moment, as though trying to figure out exactly what he was saying, and then she laughed. "You didn't read that."

"You're right. But I did want to read tonight. I thought that we could just do that together."

"So because I read, you want to too?"

"Sure. I guess maybe someday I'm hoping that you and I'll do some things on the farm together, and I figured if I wanted that, I probably ought to do some things that you wanted to do. You know, not that I think that our relationship should be equal. Sometimes you just give without getting any take, but I am giving a little, hoping for a little take."

"I think I might have been a little bit confused about the whole take and then give or give and take or not give or something, but okay."

He finished the last of his bread, and she pointed to his plate. "More?"

"I probably shouldn't, but...one more piece?"

"I think I'll have another one with you." She got up and sliced off two more pieces, bringing them back and setting his on his plate before buttering hers. "What book do you want to read?"

"I was actually going to ask you if you would pick one out for me. I enjoy things that are fast-moving. I don't want too much where they just go round and round in their head. That would drive me crazy."

"That's funny. I love books where I know exactly what the characters are thinking. In fact, I want to know every single thing they're thinking."

"Maybe that's the difference between men and women."

"Maybe. But I got it. An action book. Do you want one that's true or one that is fiction?"

"If it's fiction, it's going to have to feel true. Otherwise, I won't want it."

"So, maybe you want to start out with some nonfiction."

"Like *A Day in the Life of a Mouse*? I think maybe I'll pass on that."

She laughed. "I don't think I would recommend that to anyone, but if you would believe it, there are actually some people who check that book out and enjoy it. It's probably not my most popular book, but it's not the book that sat on the shelf for years without anyone touching it. That would be the other book that you picked out, that I didn't even know we had in this library, *Doorknobs and Their Effect on Your Life.*"

"Yeah. That was kind of forgettable."

She laughed again. "You're talking like you actually read it. We both know you didn't."

"The pictures were nice enough."

"I can only imagine."

Chapter Twenty-Four

Ryland and Lucas finished up their meal, and he helped her do the dishes, then she went out to grab a book she thought he would enjoy and actually came back with three. She insisted that he sit in her recliner, and she grabbed a blanket from a basket she had beside it and leaned against the chair at his feet. She said that she often sat on the floor because it was just more comfortable for her.

He didn't believe that for one second, except...she seemed sincere and didn't laugh, so maybe she was. At any rate, she was settled on the floor before he settled down in the recliner, figuring that if she wasn't going to use it, he would.

To his surprise, her book about a group of men who had decided to climb Mount Everest, and the reporter who went with them, chronicling their ascent, proved to be more interesting than he had imagined.

When it was 7:45, he closed the book and said, "Can I check this one out, even though the library is closed? Can I get special perks from the library?"

"You might be able to," she said, closing her book and looking at the time. "My goodness. I had no idea it was this late."

"You know, for not being a farmer, you have an interesting concept of time. There aren't too many people who don't live on ranches that would call eight o'clock late."

She laughed. "It's bedtime for me."

"I know. I told you, that's why I came early."

Her smile said she was pleased that he knew her schedule and preferences and had deliberately chosen to suit her.

"I'm gonna go check this out for you. I'll be back in a minute."

"All right. I'm going to walk out and check on Grace. See if she moved her puppies."

"Oh. I guess I kind of forgot about her."

"It's a good thing I'm here to remind you. Do I need to feed her too?"

"It's almost eight o'clock. It's time," she said cheerfully as she picked herself off the floor and carried his book out the door to the library.

He didn't know if he was causing her a whole lot of extra work by asking her to check it out for him when the library was closed, but he really did want to share her interest. Even though he had never been much of a reader.

Although, she just might convince him, because that book really was pretty good. And he was happy she had recommended it.

He supposed that meant she was good at her job.

He padded through the kitchen and opened the mudroom door carefully.

Grace had indeed moved her puppies, and when he walked out, she whined, and her tail thumped on the ground.

"Do you need to go out for a bit?" he asked.

She whined again, and he walked to the door, putting his hand on the knob.

She got up carefully, the puppies falling off with a plop onto the dog bed. It might have been just a tad bit small for a dog with puppies, but it was the best they had, and he thought it was probably better than Ryland's coat, which he wasn't sure could be salvaged or not. But he allowed Grace to walk out the door, closing it behind her, and then picked up the coat.

"She moved them!" Ryland said as she slipped out the door and into the mudroom.

"She did. And she wanted out. I... I assume that's just what you do."

"Yeah. I mean, if she were actually my dog and I knew that she would let me, I would put a collar and leash on her and walk her, but it's... I'm still not sure how much I can touch her without her biting me, and I think we already had the discussion about how neither one of us have a deep, burning desire to go to the emergency room with a dog bite this evening."

"Yeah. I kind of feel like she won't. She wagged her tail a little when I came out, but who knows where she's been or what's happened to her."

"Yeah. I have no idea what I'm going to do. But one thing I'm sure of, I won't be taking her to the humane society."

"So the library is a little small for four dogs."

"I don't know if my husband could find some people who might want a dog or not. Maybe people who have a big old ranch that has plenty of room for dogs to run on it and plenty of people to give them attention."

"Or plenty of guests who might be interested in picking up a ranch dog while they're out here on vacation."

She laughed. "I don't think that's gonna happen."

"Oh, I don't know, I think if I were to sell pigs or goats to guests, they'd take them in a heartbeat. We've had plenty of people who asked anyway."

"Interesting. Do those people know that...those animals don't live in the house?"

"We never got that far in the conversation. I just say they're not for sale. But it's kind of crazy what people think they might want and will plunk down money for."

"So now you're gonna sell my puppies?"

"Now they're your puppies? I thought we were married. Doesn't that make us one? So what's yours is mine and what's mine is yours and there is no separation of assets, unless...a dog is different?"

"Well, technically, I had the dog before I had you, so she's kind of mine."

"No. That's not how that works."

"All right. If you say so. I guess she's ours then. But that means that you're responsible for feeding her half the time."

"Are you inviting me over to your house every night this week?"

She laughed. "Really? Did you just invite yourself over?"

"No. I offered to feed our dog." He emphasized the word "our."

"I think you're a turkey."

"Now that's a good idea. Selling our guests turkeys. You are brilliant. We could raise them and have them around Thanksgiving. We could make a big deal about if they bought a turkey, they would pardon it and save it from being on someone's Thanksgiving table. You're amazing."

"I did not say that at all." She shook her head, and he realized that they laughed more tonight than they had in all the times they'd spent together. He hoped it continued.

They let Grace in, put her food and water down for her, and they walked back out to the kitchen.

He shifted from one foot to the other and wondered whether or not he should say what was on his mind.

"So are we going to meet at the courthouse tomorrow so I can move the money from my account to yours?" she asked, and he was a little disappointed, because that was not what he wanted to talk about.

"I told you, keep the money."

"Well, I'm going there, and I'm moving it. You can come or not."

"I'm going to go and see if we can get those agreements voided."

She was quiet, and then she said, "All right."

"Just like that? No argument? No fight about this? You know, we've had a relationship now for all of," he looked at his watch, "thirty-six hours. And we haven't fought once. I think it's about time."

"No. That's what you want. So that's what we'll do."

"All right." He wasn't sure what he had expected, but it wasn't her easy compliance.

"But I guess I will go to the bank and I'll add your name to my account. It's our money. It's not just mine."

"In my mind, it's yours."

"In my mind, it's ours."

"Well, I suppose we could go to the bank, and I can add you to my account as well. While we're over there."

"That's up to you."

He didn't have nearly what she had. It was hardly even worth adding her name, but...if they were together, that made things real. Sharing a bank account. He had his mom's name on his account when he first started it, because he wasn't old enough to have it in just his. But he hadn't had anyone on his bank account since his mom had passed away.

"So, you had mentioned something that you wanted."

"Yes?" she asked, shoving her hands in her pockets and looking up at him, like she was ready to talk all night. Although she did look a little tired.

He waited, and it didn't seem to occur to her exactly what he was talking about, so he figured he was going to need to spell it out, which served him right, because she had asked for it to begin with, and he hadn't realized until just then how much courage that had taken. He'd taken it for granted that she said it, and now, he admired that she managed to get the words out.

"You wanted kissing lessons."

Her eyes opened wide, and he hated that a little bit of fear crept back in them.

"But we don't have to do that if you don't want to. I just...thought I'd ask."

"Yeah. I said I wanted them."

"Do you still?" He wasn't sure what kind of impression he'd made on her this evening.

For him, she just solidified over and over in his heart and mind that she was exactly what he wanted. He enjoyed being with her, had fun laughing with her, and in fact couldn't imagine having a better evening, doing anything.

"More than ever," she said, lifting her chin and meeting his eyes.

"All right. I guess talking about it takes some of the spontaneity out of it, but...it takes a little bit of the uncertainty out too. Is that okay?"

"Spontaneity might be a good word, but uncertainty probably isn't. So fifty-fifty?" she said, raising her brows and shrugging her shoulders.

He laughed. "Maybe we don't have to dissect it quite that much. If we put percentages on it, it's...maybe not as fun."

"Maybe we could just make our own fun. We don't have to play by the rules that everyone else uses. Right?"

"I suppose you're right."

Lucas held his breath, his heart hammering in his chest. He'd said what he wanted to, what he wanted to do, but...maybe he was pushing too hard.

He reminded himself how Ryland had driven like a crazy woman to Rockerton when she learned of his plight, and how she had been willing to give her life savings for him. Everything she had planned to live on.

Suddenly the responsibility felt heavy on his shoulders. This woman had trusted him. She'd given up the security she expected to have in order to have *him*.

"Ryland, I —" He broke off. How could he tell her what he was feeling? He didn't even know. Responsibility, yes, but he felt so honored, his heart expanding in his chest, warmth flowing around and through him. He reached a hand up and touched her cheek. Her eyes closed and she leaned her head into his hand.

For some reason, he wanted to tuck her head underneath his chin and pull her close, promising that he wouldn't let anything happen to her, that he'd take care of her for the rest of her life, that she had nothing to fear.

But he didn't want to make promises he couldn't be assured he would keep. He would do all those things, of course, as much as he could.

Plus, he was supposed to be giving her kissing lessons.

Kissing lessons. That's what he thought he wanted, but he found that, while he still wanted to kiss her, he wanted more. He wanted her whole heart and soul. Her words and her soft, sweet looks, her exasperated ones too, all of them.

Ryland shifted, and his hand slid around her neck.

"I don't know what I'm supposed to do." Her voice was soft, breathy, and easy over his heart. He wanted to take it, wrap it around him, hold onto it. The sound shimmered in the air, and he had to blink his eyes, remembering what he was going to say.

"Nothing. You don't have to do anything."

"Kissing requires something," she said, a little line appearing between her brows.

He took a breath. He had told her he would give her kissing lessons. He probably should do what he said, even though he hadn't been expecting those feelings...not feeling worthy. He didn't deserve this woman. She had already sacrificed so much for him, and were kissing lessons really the only thing that he could offer her in return?

Her face fell, and under his fingers he felt her stiffen.

"If you don't want kissing, that's fine." Her voice was even softer, a little raspy, and it didn't take a rocket scientist to hear the hurt and dejection in it.

"No. That's not what I meant at all."

He took a breath. She was going to completely misunderstand if he didn't quit screwing this up. Why did he pick this time? Out of all the times in the world to finally start thinking a little deeper thoughts than just the surface ones that usually stuck in his head. His family thought he was a goofball, flitting around from friend to friend, never feeling anything deep.

He'd certainly been feeling the deep things today. Tonight, here with Ryland. She brought that out in him.

She tugged a little, like she wanted him to let her go.

"Ryland. Please. Let me explain. I..."

"No. That's fine. I didn't mean to force you to kiss me." She rolled her eyes a little, and pulled. He wanted to hold onto her, hold her tight, make her stay there until she understood, but he couldn't exactly keep her trapped in his arms.

"Ryland. Please. I... I'm no good at this. Sure, I know it seems like I should be. Because, it seems like I can talk about anything but remember our dates?"

She paused as she turned, his question about their dates making her remember that he wasn't always the smooth, easy talker that his reputation indicated, and while there was still hurt on her face, there was interest there as well. "Remember how I can talk to anyone, anywhere in the world. Anyone. I've never had the slightest bit of problem discussing anything with anyone but when you sat across from me at the table, all I could do was..."

"Shove food in your face?" she supplied helpfully.

"Yeah." They chuckled a little together, and while her face was still pinched, her shoulders didn't seem so stiff, and he felt like maybe she was relaxing.

She waited, and he tried to gather his thoughts. He wasn't used to going beyond the surface interaction.

"How many days did it take before we started talking to each other?" It was a rhetorical question, he wasn't expecting her to answer. "I... I haven't kissed a lot of girls, and I've never given kissing lessons, but it's more about the idea that you're different. Special. More than special, you made me feel things I've never felt before. And I guess I just wasn't sure... What to do. How to act, what to say, and I realized that as much as I want to kiss you, it isn't just about kissing. It was about...more." He ended with a word that he didn't really want to say. He wanted to tell her that he loved her. He was pretty sure that's what his feelings meant.

But he couldn't quite get the word out. And he thought it might be a little bit too fast.

He couldn't help but be encouraged by the fact that she had been disappointed he wasn't going to kiss her. Well, he wanted to sit and think about the idea that Ryland had been hurt and disappointed when she thought he wasn't going to kiss her.

"What are you smiling about?" she asked, leaning a little in his direction. He took a step toward her, putting his hand back around her neck, and exerting a little pressure. She came toward him willingly.

"I was smiling because I really, really like the idea that you want to kiss me."

"Why do you think I came up with the kissing lessons? And suggested them?"

"Sorry. Sometimes I'm a little dense."

"A girl doesn't want to have to do all the chasing."

"Why do you think I was in the library all of those times since this time last year? Don't you think I was chasing you there?"

"No. But I guess I figured you didn't like to read."

"I think I might. You picked out a good book for me, but it

definitely had more to do with a certain librarian and then it did for a sudden desire to start reading books on my end."

She didn't say anything, just pressed her lips together and looked up at him expectantly, like she was waiting for him... Probably because she was. She wanted kissing lessons, and she was waiting.

"So, you're standing way too far away from me in order for me to kiss you properly."

"All right. So the first rule of kissing lessons is to stand close."

"That's right. Stand close. Closer," he said as she walked forward. She wasn't touching him yet, not the whole way down her front, and so she inched closer. He tugged a little more. Wrapping an arm around her waist.

"That's almost close enough," he said with a grin, when he had her pressed completely against him.

"Now, look up."

She tilted her head, her eyes sparkling, a smile hovering around her lips.

He looked down, wondering what else there was to say. The mechanics didn't seem as important as the fact that he had her close, and she wanted him.

"And?" she asked expectantly.

"You know what?"

She tilted her head a little, but the smile on her face didn't fade. He thought maybe she believed him when he had told her that she was different than anyone else, and his hesitation didn't have anything to do with not wanting to kiss her, but more about wanting to kiss her too much. Or wanting more.

"What?" she asked.

"I think kissing is less about technique, and more about having the right person. Maybe I'm wrong. Maybe it's an odd way of thinking, but I don't really care how you kiss. It's just the idea that you're letting me kiss you. And you're kissing me back. That you're standing here in my arms, wanting to be here. Is that crazy?"

Maybe she didn't think it was, because the smile that had been teasing her lips tilted up, and her eyes glinted.

"No. I think that's perfect. That's what I was thinking anyway."

"Oh?" he asked, hoping she would expound on that.

"Yeah. For me, it doesn't really matter how you kiss. I mean, I guess if there's something really terrible about it, we could talk about it, but it's more about the idea of having the one you want. I mean, I can't imagine kissing someone that I didn't...have strong feelings for. In fact, I can't think of anyone else in the world I would like to kiss right now. Ever. Just you."

"The same for me. So much the same."

She said it better than he ever could have.

"Does this mean I don't get kissing lessons?" she asked, her brow raised.

"Maybe kissing lessons might turn out to be less about lessons and more about practicing. After all, it is important that you stand close, and it's important that you have the right one, and beyond that, I think it's just whatever works for the two of us."

"I think I like that kind of lesson. And I can get on board with that."

"Good thing. Because I can, too."

He breathed in her scent, fresh and clean and serious with a little kick of humor. He'd found she was funny and she smiled easily, but she definitely did have a serious streak, a quiet, contemplative type of personality, where she thought about things. He had a tendency to act rather than think. Maybe they would be compatible in that area. Or he would encourage her to be more impulsive, and she would encourage him to stop and think.

He lowered his head, brushed his lips across her temple.

"You smell perfect."

"I think that's a good thing?" she said, rubbing her cheek against his, and putting her lips to the corner of his jaw.

He wasn't sure his heart could take an actual kiss, after the way it was acting with just her lips on his jaw. His fingers tightened around her, and he had to remind himself to relax. He didn't want to grip her so hard he hurt her.

"Yeah."

She was warm and soft under his fingers, and his lips trailed down along her cheek.

Her eyes closed, and he found his closing as well. Kissing was better experienced when a person's eyes were closed so they could feel more than they saw.

He shifted, his head moving just a bit, and she seemed to naturally move with him, until his lips settled over hers, soft and warm and exactly right.

Maybe he'd been a little nervous about kissing her. Maybe he had been concerned that it was their first kiss and he wanted it to be perfect, but he wasn't thinking about any of that now. He was just caught up in the way she felt, the way she smelled, the way she moved under his hands and mouth.

He wasn't sure how the kiss deepened, or how long he stood there, he just knew his knees were weak, and he wanted, wanted desperately, for her to ask him to stay.

But even if she did, he knew he would need to say no. Their relationship was too new and it was too soon for them to move on to more physical things when they still had to build something more solid first. Or at least, that's what he tried to tell his fuzzy brain as he lifted his head and rested his temple beside hers, her breath in his ear, her hand sliding down his back, her heartbeat just as loud and fast as his.

"I think kissing you might be dangerous to my health." He didn't mean that as an insult, and he was gratified when she huffed out a little laugh.

"And here I thought it was you that was dangerous to mine. Is that the way kissing always feels?"

"I don't know. Not for me. Never for me." And that was the absolute truth. He couldn't even remember the kissing that he'd done before her. He wished there wasn't anything to remember at all, but maybe that was the way the Lord did it. It all fled his mind, paled in comparison to the woman he currently held in his arms. She was so perfect for him, and he couldn't believe not only were they together, but they were actually married.

But he wanted to do it right with her. Develop a relationship with her, however he did that, maybe by learning to talk to her a little bit, but also by being together. Working together. That's what his parents had said. That if you work with someone, you really get to know them, because you'd see them during the worst of times, you'd see whether or not they were diligent, and get a really good glimpse of their character.

"Will you come out to the farm with me?" he asked, and noted that his voice still sounded a little breathless.

"Now?" she asked, surprise in her tone, her fingers still holding on to him tightly.

"No. The next time you can. The library is closed on Mondays, right?"

"Yeah."

"Then Monday? Will you spend some time on the farm with me? I want to show you where I live, what I do. I want you to see the place that I love."

"That's fair, because you've been here, at the place I love."

"Yeah." And she was right. He hadn't even thought about it, but he had naturally wanted to share what she loved - the library, books, reading. He hoped that she would learn to love the ranch the way he did.

"To be on the ranch with you. I know you enjoy the work there, being with your siblings, and I'd really love to be a part of it, if I can."

"There are always jobs for people to do. If we go out there, it's more than likely that someone's going to grab you, then put you in charge of something. Just be ready for that, but I can try to get us out of it if you're not interested."

"I would love that! It would make me feel...like a part of your family."

"You are part of my family." He put both hands on her shoulders, and lifted her head, looking into her eyes. "We're married. That means my family is yours. And they know it. They'll do anything for you. The same way they'll do anything for me."

She smiled, almost as though humoring him, and said, "If you say so."

"I do. That's the way families are."

"Not necessarily," she said, brows lifted.

"That's the way my family is. If you haven't noticed, we're a little different."

"I have noticed." She smiled then, and he smiled back, and he knew he probably should just leave, but he said, "What about a goodbye kiss?"

"Someone told me I should do lots of practicing. That sounds like a good excuse to practice."

"Yeah. Someone very wise must have suggested doing that...as long as the only one you practice on is me."

"You don't have to worry about that," she said, as his lips lowered to hers, and they practiced their goodbye kiss.

Chapter Twenty-Five

"So...have you guys decided what you're doing?" the woman at the desk said, looking up at them, brows raised, barely contained impatience on her face.

Ryland lifted her chin. She was determined that Lucas was going to get the money.

"Yes." She spoke just as Lucas shifted. He cleared his throat.

"I won't accept a deposit and if you give me a check, I'm not cashing it."

"What you two do between yourselves is up to you." The lady pointed at the papers. "If you're going to sign, you need to sign. You had all weekend to think about it."

"I think we can rip those papers up," Lucas said. He lifted his brows at Ryland, who nodded.

The paper said that he had gotten the money. And that he agreed to stay married to her for five years in exchange for them. She didn't want him to stay married to her because he signed some paper saying he got money in exchange for it. But she did want him to take the money.

They already had all of her bank account information, but he had told her he didn't want the transaction to go through. The lady at the desk had been floored, but she had allowed them to talk it out. At least to a point.

Ryland wanted the money to just go into his account, and then she wouldn't have to think about it. But he wouldn't take it and he wouldn't sign the paper stating that he had. Because that would be a lie. It wasn't that he didn't want to stay married for five years. At least he said that several times over.

Ryland's issue was that she knew the ranch needed the money. Knew the point of Lucas selling himself was for the sole reason of trying to save the ranch. If he refused the money, the whole exercise would have been in vain. Except, it hadn't been. Because she was married to a good man, a man she planned to spend the rest of her life with, a man she believed she loved.

She definitely loved kissing him too. She thought about their goodbye kiss for the entire day yesterday. He'd taken her to church, they had a quiet lunch at her apartment, and checked on Grace and the puppies before she'd open the library.

He had gone home because he had chores to do at the ranch and she hadn't seen him again.

Now, it was Monday morning and she honestly wanted to get this part of the day over as quickly as possible, because she was going to be spending the rest of the day with him at the ranch, and she had been looking forward to that, almost as much as she'd been looking forward to more kissing lessons. Or, maybe more accurately, more practicing.

She signed the paper to allow the transaction to pay the auction company to go through. They would take their cut no matter whether Lucas got money.

"So you want this agreement to be destroyed?" the lady said, holding up the agreement, in her two fingers.

"Yes." They spoke at the same time, then glanced at each other. Ryland smiled, but she was also a little bit annoyed. Why did he have to be too proud to take her money?

They were heading toward the ranch, she could talk to his oldest brother, Ezra. Maybe he could talk some sense into him.

They finished up at the courthouse, with Lucas taking her hand as they walked away, the paper they were supposed to sign shredded in the garbage can behind them.

"That worked out well," Lucas said, coming out of the courthouse, holding the door while she stepped down as well. He took her hand again, and they lifted their faces to the deep blue North Dakota sky.

"Maybe for you. I'm frustrated."

"I'm sorry. I know I can be annoying at times, but there's just no way I can take your money. Like you're paying me to marry you. Don't you remember how upset you were Saturday night when you thought I was just kissing you because I had to and that I didn't actually want to kiss you? How do you think this is going to affect our relationship if we get mad at each other, which is almost certainly going to happen. People don't constantly get along without arguing and fussing at some point, and you're going to feel like maybe I only married you for your money. You know?"

"I suppose you could be right," she said softly, knowing he absolutely was. That was exactly something that she would think when she was upset and not sure of how he felt. "Am I allowed to say that I'm surprised you even considered that? It doesn't seem like something you'd think about."

"It's not. But maybe being around you has caused me to stop talking so much, and start thinking a little more."

"Really?" she said, laughing a little because she didn't think for one second that she had that kind of influence on him.

But he wasn't smiling.

"Yeah, really. You...influence me for sure."

They started down the steps, the town of Rockerton coming awake around them. It was shortly after nine, and while the streets weren't busy, an occasional car motored by, and there were several people walking on the sidewalks.

Stores were opening, and it felt like a beautiful day to be alive. Like everyone was smiling, or maybe that was just her heart being happy. It was true that she was a little frustrated, but it was also true that her frustration stemmed from the fact that Lucas didn't want to take advantage of her, and that made her feel like their relationship was more important than saving the ranch he loved, even though it would benefit his siblings. He was obviously putting her first. Ahead of even his family, which she knew he loved with all his heart.

They arrived at his truck, and he opened her door for her. It made her smile, that gallant and gentlemanly gesture.

So much like the hero of a romance novel.

"Thank you," she murmured as she slipped into her seat, setting her purse beside her.

"My pleasure," he said as he closed the door and walked around.

He got in and drove out of Rockerton. She had been enjoying the companionable silence between them, before he spoke. "So if there was something that you could do on the ranch, do you have a preference? Do you like to cook? I assume you don't ride horses? Would you like to work with the cows? To learn how to do anything?"

"I hadn't considered that," she said, knowing it was true. He had said that they would grab her and give her a job, but she hadn't stopped to think too much about what kind of job it might be. The idea that his family would accept her and treat her like one of them made her heart happy.

She'd never really felt like part of her own family. Especially since her mother had gotten remarried. Not that she begrudged her mother any kind of happiness. Honestly she was happy for her, happy that she seemed to enjoy her second family. It was just... She never really felt like she fit in, and the idea of fitting in with Lucas's family made her a little giddy inside.

After thinking about it a little bit, she realized she really had no clue. "What are my choices? I mean, you're right, I can't ride a horse, and I suppose that I'd like to learn, but I know I won't be able to do it well enough to actually have a job that requires that skill. Not for a while anyway. Maybe not ever. The idea is a little scary."

"It can be a little bit scary to be on the back of something that you don't have total and complete control over. But, there is also a definite feeling of freedom and enjoyment that you can only get from the back of the horse. An ATV just isn't quite the same."

"It's not as noble anyway," she said with a laugh.

He chuckled as well. "Exactly. Although, sometimes an ATV can get away from you as well, but in that case you have no one to blame but yourself."

"I doubt that will happen with me. I drove to Rockerton faster than I've ever driven anywhere before in my life, and I have no desire to repeat the experience. I'm pretty happy with my old lady putting along speed."

"You don't look like a real daredevil to me, but I've learned a few things about you that were surprising, so I'm sure there's going to be more layers as I get to know you."

"Well I hope so. I hope there's a little bit more depth to me rather than just a mousey old librarian."

"Hey. Don't talk about my wife like that. You're not mousey, and you're definitely not old, but you are a really awesome librarian."

She smiled at his defense of her, feeling it the whole way to her bones. She wasn't used to having someone defend her, or to tell her that she was awesome in anything. She just wasn't the kind of person people looked at and saw anything worth complementing. But Lucas had taken the time to see her, to know her, and she loved that he wasn't afraid to say kind things to her.

"I like babies but I bet probably everybody else does too."

"We often fight over who gets to take care of the babies. And yeah, it's the most fun job, in my opinion anyway. Although, I like driving tractors too."

"You can have that job. I'm not interested. I can barely drive my car." She thought she was rather a good driver, but she didn't have any interest in getting behind the wheel of the tractor and being responsible for that kind of power and weight.

"I actually think you'd be a really good tractor driver. I think I should show you how."

"So there are no jobs with the babies."

"We have some new goats. We just got them not long ago, thinking that the dude ranch guests would enjoy them. They're a huge hit with our visitors, but I don't think anyone is in charge of taking care of them." He looked across the seat at her, then glanced back at the road. "It would be a daily job."

"You mean I would have to come out to the ranch every day?"

"Yeah."

He didn't say anything else, and she closed her mouth around the words that wanted to come out. He hadn't said anything about her moving in with him. Or, even about him moving in with her.

She hoped it was because he wanted them to get to know each other a little bit before they move forward with the physical side of their relationship, but he hadn't said, and she wasn't sure. She kind of thought that since they were married, they should be living together, but maybe he didn't have plans for them to ever live together, and that look he'd had given her didn't mean anything.

"Right now with Grace..." Her voice trailed off. It didn't take that long to take care of the dog and the puppies. Maybe she should think about moving them out to the ranch. "Actually, never mind. I could get up and go to the ranch every day."

"Now that I'm thinking about it, it probably would need to be twice a day. The goats are in a pen and small enclosure, not out in the pasture where they can eat to their heart's content. So they need to be fed twice a day." He eyed her again, and she couldn't read the look on his face. "I'd love it if you do it, but that might be a little bit much. Closing the library in the evening and then running out to the ranch. It would be well past your eight o'clock bedtime before you got to bed at night, especially on the nights when the library closes late."

"Yeah." Her mind ran around the possibilities. She wanted to help. She wanted to be a part of the ranch, and getting to work with the baby goats was a dream job. Goats wouldn't be so big that they would scare her, unlike cattle. Although babies wouldn't be bad, a baby cow had a mama cow that was much bigger than she was comfortable with. Especially considering that she'd never been around cows before.

"I don't want to commit to something and not be able to do it."

"Animals depend on us to feed them, and if we don't come through, or don't do what we need to do, then they don't get fed. So I appreciate your consideration, and not jumping into something that you aren't sure you can keep up with."

The expression on his face warmed her heart. She thought he really meant that. That he admired her for counting the cost, in Bible speak. It was making sure that a person was willing to make the sacrifice that they were committing to and to stick with their commitments.

Sometimes she didn't do that. Sometimes she did bite off more than she could chew, but that was more because she liked to make big goals, and sometimes she didn't quite hit what she was aiming for. But, if a person attempted big goals, at least they had something to show for it, even if they didn't quite get what they were aiming for. If they didn't have goals to begin with, if they didn't even try, they would never know what they might have been capable of.

Of course, up until this point in her life, most of her big goals involved seeing how many books she could read in a year, or month, or even a day. They didn't involve taking another life and committing to the care of it.

Maybe she was taking it too seriously. She was married to the man who lived on the ranch. She wanted to be there. This would give her an excuse, just in case Lucas stopped coming to the library.

Her heart gave a sharp pang at the thought. Was that what was going to happen? Now that he had her, would he stop being interested? It wasn't that she necessarily wanted him to chase after her constantly, but she supposed there was a part of her that wanted to know that he was still interested in her, interested enough to go out of his way to want to be with her.

She told herself to stop overthinking, and just commit.

"I'll do it. You show me what to do, and I'll be there morning and night to feed the goats."

There. It wasn't that hard. Now she had a job on the farm, something to draw her there morning and night, and she would get to know Lucas's world a little bit. After all, he'd been the one to step out of his comfort zone and come into hers. The best thing she could do would be to step into his, and learn what he needed her to, in order for her to become a part of the things that he loved.

His eyes glinted as he glanced across the seat at her, the smile on his face big and real. "That's my girl."

A thrill went down her backbone. It was crazy that something as simple as having him call her "his girl" would make her feel so good. But it did. She wanted to think that she belonged to him, and that he also belonged to her. Of course, that's what marriage meant, but until they actually lived what they said they were going to, it didn't really feel real.

"I told my siblings that you and I would be out today, hanging around, and checking things out. Hopefully they won't put us to work. But, don't be totally surprised if we get there and there's some kind of job that needs to be done, and they're grabbing the nearest people and throwing them on it."

"All right. I won't be surprised. I might not be much help to them, though."

"You're going to do just fine." The confidence in his voice made her feel confident as well.

"So tell me about your family," she said, and she just wanted to hear him talk and maybe help her get prepared for what she was going to face at the barn. She had always been quiet, unassuming, willing to be in the background. She'd never had a big loud, crazy family bustling around her. She had to admit, it was a little intimidating, especially coupling that with the fact that they were going to be on the ranch, doing things that she didn't know how to do, and didn't even know if she could do. Her palms felt sweaty, and she resisted the urge to rub them against her legs.

"You know Ezra is the oldest. He's always been very bossy, commanding if you will, but he means well. And Alaska has softened him. That's his wife, and you know them from church."

"Yeah. And I guess I could tell that Ezra was rather commanding as well."

"I think you also know Tobias. He is a lot different than Ezra, but he still commands respect. Just in a different way."

"He's not married."

"And I doubt he'd ever get married. He... There are just some things that happened to him, and...maybe someday we can talk about that. But it's too heavy for today."

"All right."

"He's been helping Mrs. Wells whose farm is a little north of ours. He's just always doing things quietly, never tooting his horn, but he dispenses wisdom as well, and if Tobias speaks, people have a tendency to listen."

"That's a huge compliment."

"It sure is." He turned the turn signal on and slowed as they came up on the lane to the ranch. "I have the highest respect for him."

He kept talking as they pulled down the lane. "You'll probably see Joanna and Stonewall. They are inseparable. They've been best friends since forever, and Stonewall even moved here with our family when we moved from Wyoming. He and Joanna do everything together."

"But they're just friends?" Ryland said, finding it a little unbelievable that someone would move hundreds of miles just to continue to be with a friend, when there wasn't anything more involved.

"You'll see. We all think that eventually there will be something more, but nobody ever says anything to them, and they're oblivious to the fact that they would be perfect together."

"Or maybe it's the idea that they don't want to rock the boat. When you have something that good, sometimes it's hard to take the chance of upsetting the status quo, and losing something you truly value."

He nodded, the look on his face saying that he thought she had hit the nail on the head.

"I think you're exactly right about them."

A little part of her wanted to see if she could do something that would set the two of them up, but she didn't want to do anything that could end up separating them. It wasn't like she had a solid position in the family, where she could make a mistake of major proportions. She tried to push the matchmaking side of herself away as Lucas pulled into the parking area beside the big house.

"You ready?"

She tried not to look as nervous as she felt. "Yes."

Truly, she was excited to step into his world. Grateful that she had the opportunity, and hopeful she could make the best of it.

Chapter Twenty-Six

Ryland took a deep breath. It seemed busy, almost busier on the ranch than it had in Rockerton. There were people walking to the barn, people walking from the barn, and as she got out of the truck, several ladies stepped out of the house, followed by a tall, serious looking man. Ezra. The oldest, and most likely the one with the biggest burden on his shoulders.

Fingering the piece of paper that she'd taken out of her purse, she didn't wait for Lucas, but strode up the steps. She knew Ezra from church, although she didn't talk to him on a regular basis.

"Hi, Alaska," she greeted the small woman beside him. The marks of a hard life were written on her skin, but her smile was genuine and happy, and she looked years younger than she had when she had first come to church.

"Welcome. I was hoping when I heard that Lucas had managed to get you to marry him, that he would also manage to get you out here on the ranch."

"I wanted to come. I'm excited to be here, although I'm a little nervous as well." She figured she might as well be honest.

She turned her gaze to Ezra and held out the check she'd written out earlier. "I wanted to give you this. Lucas wouldn't take it, but I understood that he was in the auction because the ranch needed it."

Ezra did not move to take the check.

She lifted her brow and gritted her jaw.

"You can argue with me if you want to, but I'm going to insist."

To her astonishment, a corner of Ezra's mouth curled up. "I can see what Lucas sees in you," he said, throwing her even more off-balance. She hadn't expected a personal statement, or anything along those lines. Maybe he would deny needing it, or maybe he would thank her, but... He almost seemed to be saying that he found something in her to like. This family was going to be terrible for her ego.

She didn't really think that. But she did appreciate being around people who saw good in her, and weren't afraid to talk about it.

"I tried to tell you," Alaska said, looking up at her husband with a lifted brow. The child that stood at her feet, clung to her leg and occasionally peeked out from behind it, looking Ryland over as though unsure what to think about the stranger who stood on her porch.

"You were right," Ezra said.

For some reason that made Alaska laugh, and they shared a look that people who were deeply in love often shared. It made Ryland smile.

She wanted to look at Lucas and see what he thought about the situation, but he was standing a little behind her and she didn't want to be obvious about it. However, she felt his hand on the small of her back, as though he were thinking about her, and wanted to make sure that she knew it through the touch of his fingers. Whatever it was, she appreciated that little bit of contact.

"Thank you for this," Ezra said, holding up the check. "Although the only way I will take it is if you consider it a loan."

"That's fine. But I'm not charging interest, and there are no terms for repayment." She made her words sound firm and final. It wasn't something she was going to negotiate about.

As though he understood, Ezra nodded once, and then said, "Fair enough. Now, has Lucas given you a job yet? Or do I need to grab you and put you to work?"

"He told me that maybe I could be responsible for the goats."

"I was actually going to suggest that!" Alaska exclaimed. "Since we've gotten them, we've all kind of taken turns taking care of them, and they're super sweet and really cute, but someone needs to be the point person." Alaska smiled, as though the idea of Ryland being on the farm made her happy. Which went a long way toward making Ryland feel at home. "And so you don't feel too much pressure, anyone around the farm will be absolutely happy to help you out. Taking care of those baby goats is not a hardship." She paused. "Unless you're moving out here?"

Ryland took a breath, her mouth open. But she didn't know what to say. Without conscious thought, her head turned toward Lucas and she lifted her brows.

"I guess it's something we need to talk about." He didn't seem nearly as uncomfortable as she felt. She supposed it was a natural question, and Alaska was not attacking them, or demanding, or even judging them because of their choices. It was obvious she was just curious, which was fine.

Ryland herself was curious.

Alaska huffed out a small laugh like she thought it was funny. Maybe it was.

"All right," Ezra said. "If Lucas has a job for you, and you guys are busy, go ahead. Enjoy the day. It's a beautiful one."

"Are you sticking around for supper?" Alaska asked.

Again, Ryland wasn't sure what to say. So again, she turned to Lucas, to defer to him.

"Yeah. If it's okay with Ryland. I think it'll be good for us to sit down. Although, maybe it depends on how intimidated she is by everyone. There are a lot of us."

"Sure are. And you guys can be a little intimidating. It's loud and crazy, especially when you're not used to it."

Ryland felt like she would have a kindred spirit in Alaska. Someone else who had come into the family, and from the way it looked, they had accepted her, and she felt at home. Of course, it probably helped to have her husband standing beside her.

"All right. You heard them. Let's go figure out how to feed those goats."

She laughed, taking the hand Lucas offered, and feeling a lot lighter going down the stairs than she had when she'd gone up.

That hadn't been so bad. They'd actually acted like they liked her, not that she had expected anything less, she just...hadn't been sure what to expect. And sometimes, families could circle the wagons, so to speak, and make a newcomer feel like an outsider for a really long time. She didn't think the Clybourns were like that, from seeing them at church, but sometimes people weren't always the way they seem.

"That was a great welcome. I hope it's all that easy."

"Really? Ezra is probably one of the stuffiest of my siblings. Although Alaska is nice. Not sure what she sees in him, but he's better since she's around. She makes him a little softer."

"I think that's what women are supposed to do for men," Ryland said, and then she felt her cheeks heat, because she hadn't been thinking necessarily about her impact on Lucas. But from the grin that he threw at her, he had been.

"I don't know. I'm not sure I want to get any softer," he said, patting his stomach.

"I'm not a fantastic cook, so I don't think you really have to worry about that."

"I don't know. That stew was pretty good."

She laughed. Because there wasn't anything special about the stew, and he certainly wasn't going to get fat or soft on it.

"Over that way are the outbuildings that we fixed up for the dude ranch. We have some folks staying here right now, and I love to mingle, but Mondays are usually a slow day."

"They are at the library too. That's why it's closed today."

"I figured. Probably gets busier over the weekends, same way the dude ranch does. People getting off work, and heading out to do some fun things with their family."

"Did you just call going to the library a fun thing?" she asked, her tone teasing.

"I did, didn't I?" he said, acting like it was an accident, when she knew better.

He talked about the horses as they walked by them, introducing her to a couple of them, and then motioned beyond them to the far pasture, where she could see a herd of black and brown cattle grazing.

He pointed out the implement shed, and they passed several of his siblings who were friendly and welcoming. Asher even thanked her for marrying Lucas, implying with his tone that Lucas wouldn't have been able to find anyone else who would take him.

While it was funny, she had the strongest urge to defend Lucas, because he was most definitely a good catch. Kind, considerate, and willing to sacrifice if necessary. He didn't make her feel like it was a sacrifice though. Like he really wanted to do whatever it took to make her smile. He was charming, and she was most definitely falling for him.

Not to mention he was a great kisser. Not that she would have mentioned that to Asher.

"And here is the shed where we keep the goats. Around back there is a small fenced area for them where they can get out and run around. Eventually we'd like to make it a little bigger, and expand our herd, but for now, we have six nanny goats."

"Do they all have babies?" she asked, remembering that they'd said something about baby goats.

"They do. Most of them are four to six weeks old, although we just had a set of triplets born two weeks ago. They're so adorable."

And he was adorable saying the word adorable. She kept that thought to herself as he opened the door, and she walked into the sweet smelling building. Hay, a deep, nurturing scent that she assumed was the feed, and the goat smell itself, musky and earthy, filled the building.

"We should have gone around back. They're all outside," Lucas said, as they saw that the pen inside was indeed empty.

They walked back out and turned around the corner of the building. Ryland tilted her head just a little, thinking that something didn't quite look right.

She figured it out as Lucas said, "They're out."

He turned to Ryland while pulling his phone out of his pocket and sending off a couple of quick texts.

"Guess you're going to get baptized by fire today."

"I'm not sure what that means, but it sounds a little scary," she said, her brow pushed in.

He sighed, hit send, clicked his phone off and shoved it in his pocket.

"It means, sometimes chasing animals can get a little hairy, but it's a necessary evil on the farm. No fence is one hundred percent perfect, and there will almost always be days where animals get out. Usually a Sunday morning, or some other time when you have plans, and don't have time to mess with them."

They stepped around a pile of old boards that sat beside the new shed.

"I'm not sure who left those there, but be careful. I see some nails poking out." He frowned at the pile of boards. "That was not a good place to leave those."

"I'll be careful."

"All right. I've got some help on the way. One of the good things about having a large family. But until they get here, I'm going to open the gate, and then we're going to try to just funnel the animals back in. We don't want to scare them so they run further away. That would be the most important thing."

"All right. There's nothing to be afraid of, right? I mean, the mothers aren't going to attack me or anything?"

"No. And even if they do, they weigh less than you do, well most of them do. Regardless, they might be bigger than you, but they're not going to hurt you. I can...almost promise that."

"I don't like the lack of confidence in your tone."

"Yeah. I guess I just kept thinking about the time I tell you that nothing's going to happen, something will. You know that's how it goes."

"Yeah. I guess it is." That was true for anywhere, not just the ranch.

Phoebe came jogging over. "The goats got out?" she huffed as she stopped beside them.

No one needed to answer, because her eyes were on the mama goats with their babies, casually walking toward the big vegetable garden behind the implement shed.

"Wow. We better get those quickly, or Alaska and Claudia are going to have my hide."

"They'll be pretty upset if the goats undo all the work they put in the garden so far this year."

"Did you get a plan together?" Joanna, a younger sister, said as she came up. Her best friend, the one that Lucas had been talking about, Stonewall, followed her.

Ryland knew all of them a little bit from church, but Joanna was a good bit younger than she was, and they hardly ever spoke.

"Oh, hi Ryland. Thanks for buying Lucas. We were worried he was going to go to some ax murderer in Siberia or something."

"Worried, or hopeful?" Stonewall said, winking at Ryland, and giving Lucas a look that said they were almost as close as brothers, if not closer.

"Maybe you guys could stop making fun of me, and start helping. Would that be too much to ask?" Lucas said as he motioned Phoebe on toward the far side of the goats, effectively telling her to cut them off and turn them around.

"You two make sure that they don't run in either direction, and if you can stand here," he said to Ryland, "And just make sure they turn the corner and go right in the gate there."

"Okay," she said, trying to put some confidence in that word. Confidence that she didn't feel. From the way he was arranging things, it looked to her like the goats were going to be coming straight toward her, and she was going to have to make them do a right angle turn. She wasn't sure her goat herding skills were up to the task. They had never been utilized before.

If it had been a bunch of first-graders heading toward the library shelves, she could have told them what direction to go, and gotten them where they needed to be.

Goats surely couldn't be that much harder than first-graders.

She eyed the animals, and revised her opinion. She'd take first-graders any day.

But these goats were going to be hers, so she needed to be brave, and more than that, she didn't want to fail the first test she had on the farm.

Phoebe had made it to the head goat, and while the goat was not scary, and didn't run away, it maybe was a little bit too friendly, because Phoebe fought to get her to turn.

"Turn around, you silly girl," Phoebe said.

Just at that moment, someone down by the implement shed started one of the old tractors that Ryland had noticed earlier. It backfired, sounding like a gunshot reverberating across the ranch grounds.

The goat was already turning, and the gunshot made everything go faster. Not only did she turn, she kicked her heels, and started running directly toward Ryland. Joanna and Stonewall and Lucas were on either side, keeping all six of the goats inline so they made a beeline toward her.

She felt a lot of pressure as she waited for them to get a little closer before she started to wave her arms. She didn't want to stop them and have them go in the wrong direction again. But, she didn't want them to run through her, either.

As they got about 20 feet away, she lifted her hands and waved them, saying, "That way. Go that way."

Hopefully she was doing it right. For a long second, maybe two, she was afraid she wasn't. The goats continued toward her, then, at the last moment, the front one swerved, jumping into the pen. Two of the other larger goats followed it. The babies weren't quite as quick, but they were very agile. They jumped right around Ryland, and went about ten feet before they realized their mothers weren't with them.

Ryland wasn't sure whether she should stand and continue to try to wave the rest of the goats into the pen, or chase the little ones so they didn't get away.

She noticed that Lucas seemed to be having a little bit of difficulty with some of the babies who wanted to take off in his direction, and Phoebe had one more mama that didn't want to turn. It didn't seem to be fazed by the backfiring of the tractor or the low rumble that now sounded in the distance.

So, Ryland turned, and hurried toward the babies that had gone past her. Maybe she could get them turned around quickly, and headed in the right direction before the rest of the goats made it to her.

The babies had jumped up on the pile of old lumber that sat there, the one Lucas had not been very happy about. Remembering that he said that there were nails in them, she tried to shoo the babies off as gently as she could, hoping they didn't get hurt.

Two of them jumped off just fine, but the other one jumped to one side, jumped to the other, and then seemed to do a flip in midair, turning around and coming straight toward her.

She instinctively lunged to try to catch it, but her foot caught on a piece of one of the two by fours that were sticking out, and she went down hard, her leg catching on something and a sharp pain traveling up her forearm.

She tried to move her arm, tried to get back up, but while her legs would move, her arm felt like it was stuck. That's when she looked down and realized that a nail was stuck in the fleshy part of her forearm while blood oozed out of a ragged cut in her leg.

Chapter Twenty-Seven

"I am so sorry!" Phoebe said yet again as Ryland got to her feet after Lucas had counted to three and pulled her arm off the nail. She winced, gingerly holding her arm in an awkward angle. It wasn't even her arm that was the major problem. She had somehow scraped her leg on another nail, and they'd wrapped it with a clean cloth, determining that it was going to need stitches.

"It's okay. I promise. Lucas had said today was going to be a trial by fire. I just didn't realize that that was code speak for you're going to be going to the emergency room later today."

Phoebe tried to laugh. She appreciated the fact that Ryland had a sense of humor, and wasn't crying or upset, or worse, wasn't having hysterics. Or threatening to sue. But still, she had been the one to put those boards there, when she knew full well they had nails sticking out of them, and they should have been taken care of right away. She had just needed to hurry inside to finish the cooking so that the guests had food to eat last night, and she had forgotten about it this morning in all the hustle and bustle of everything else that she needed to do.

"Seriously, sis. I mean, I don't like the fact that Ryland and I are making a trip to the ER, but you know that this stuff happens. If it hadn't been this, maybe she would have fallen and hurt herself worse somehow. Don't sweat it, okay?"

"Thanks," she said to Lucas, still feeling bad. But grateful that he wasn't upset either. Sometimes men could get very possessive and protective of their wives, especially newlyweds, and Lucas hadn't been married for very long.

"Sure thing, sis," he said, wrapping his arm around Ryland, then putting his other arm around her knees and scooping her up.

She protested, but he insisted, and their laughter carried back to Phoebe as he carried Ryland toward his truck.

She smiled, happy that Lucas had found someone to be with him, and thrilled that they were so much in love. But there was a part of her that was sad too. She had devoted her life to her family, although maybe not completely intentionally. After all, she had dreams at one point of falling in love and getting married and having a family of her own. But, her parents' accident, and their death, had changed all of that. She and her twin sister Priscilla, were the oldest girls in the family and although Ezra had shouldered as much as he could, they couldn't allow him to have all the responsibility resting on him.

She picked up an armful of the boards, and carried them toward the pile behind the barn, where they would be well out of the way, and no one would fall and get hurt on them.

Would she do things differently if she could go back? Would she take on the responsibility of her family, raising her siblings, and give up the opportunity that she had to have a family of her own?

At thirty-six, there wasn't much hope left that she would get married.

Her twin sister, Priscilla, had married, but she regretted it. Her marriage had been a disaster, and while she had two beautiful children from it, her spouse and she were constantly fighting over the kids.

She sighed, walking back and getting another armful of wood. She knew she wouldn't change a thing. Her family meant everything to her, and if that meant that she never got married, then so be it. She wouldn't leave the people that she loved high and dry to pursue her own happiness. Especially when happiness was such an elusive thing, and she wasn't guaranteed that what she found would make her happy.

Plus, happiness was a choice. She found it in the Lord. She had to remind herself of that. Doing His work, His will, even if that meant giving up what she wanted, and surrendering to what God wanted for her was truly the only thing that would give her the life she wanted. After all, God wanted the best for her, and He alone knew what that was.

There was no doubt in her mind about that.

The big yellow bus pulled up as she carried the last armful of boards to behind the shed, and she came out from around the corner to see Mina, the girl who had been living with them for the last year, as her parents had separated, and then divorced, in a very ugly and nasty way, get off the bus.

She smiled as Mina came running over, her backpack slapping against her back, her eyes bright with excitement.

"Aunt Phoebe! Aunt Phoebe! I need you to do something for me!" She stopped in front of Phoebe, panting, no idea that Phoebe's day had not been going very well, and that Ryland, her newest aunt, had been carried off the property, bleeding.

Phoebe wouldn't break that news to her right away. She wasn't even sure that Mina had met Ryland as Lucas's wife, although she knew that Mina had seen her at church.

"What can I do for you, honey?" she asked, smiling. There was no need to ask whether she had a good day at school. Her shining eyes and smiling face said that she had.

"We have a fundraiser that we are doing, and I need to get someone to go to jail for me."

"Go to jail? Did you do something wrong? Do you have something you want to tell me?"

"No. Silly. This is a fundraiser. I make so much money for every hour this person spends in jail, and I can do it myself, except, I have state orchestra the day that I'm scheduled to be in the jail. So I'll get the donations, I'll get people to pledge money, but I need you to go to jail for me."

"Wow. I don't know if I love you that much," Phoebe said, with a silly grin that made Mina laugh.

"I know you do. You're the first one I thought of. You'll do anything for me. I mean, I know everyone else loves me too, but you're the first person to do whatever I need. So, going to jail is not exactly a little thing. I wasn't sure about Ezra, and also he needs to be here to run the ranch, but I knew that you would."

"Well you're right. I've never gone to jail for anyone, but I will make you my first exception. Although, this is not going on my permanent record, is it?"

Mina's brow scrunched up. "I don't think so. Do you want me to ask tomorrow?"

"No. I know it's not. I was just mostly teasing you. I'll need to know what day, so I can take off, and be sure that I'm able to get there. Do you have a certain time? Do you have a paper or something with all the information?"

"I have a QR code that you can scan, and it'll tell you everything you need to know on the website."

Of course. Phoebe had been homeschooled, and she'd never gone to school, but even when she was younger, everything had been on paper. Although, the older she got, the more likely it was that there were going to be emails and websites and electronically passed information. That seemed to be all anyone did anymore. Welcome to the new world, she supposed.

She pulled her phone out of her pocket, and scanned the QR code that Mina held up from a card she pulled from her bookbag.

"If you have any questions, I can go to school and ask my teacher."

"Alright. I can do this. It's a Friday night into Saturday, and I just have to make sure that I can get off."

"I knew you would! Thank you!" Mina said, wrapping her arms around Phoebe, and squeezing tight.

Phoebe's heart squeezed, her eyes pricking a little with tears. This is the way her younger siblings used to be with her. After their parents had died, particularly their mom, they felt bereft and sad, of course. Phoebe had been the one who had been there for them. She made sure that they cleaned their rooms, washed their clothes, did their chores, and that their schoolwork was done as well. She taught the classes she needed to, and basically took over her mom's spot.

Sometimes she missed the role of sister. Because she felt more like a mom, especially to Lois who was the youngest. But, she wouldn't trade it for anything. Because she had the opportunity to shape and mold her siblings.

Now she had Mina.

She wasn't going to ask God why he hadn't given her a family of her own. He had other people who needed her.

And, while she longed for a spouse, a significant other, someone to share her hopes and dreams and life with, that just wasn't the way God had directed her life. She had to trust that it was for the best.

"I love you," Mina said, pulling back and looking up at Phoebe with such a beautiful smile on her face, that Phoebe found herself blinking back tears again.

"I love you, too. And thank you for allowing me to take your place in jail. It's an honor."

She smiled as she said it, being a little bit sarcastic, but meaning it as well. She could have asked anyone, and she'd come directly to Phoebe. That meant something.

With their arms around each other, they started toward the house, Mina chattering on about her day and her friends and the music that she needed to practice before she went to state orchestra.

As they walked in the house, through the living room into the kitchen, Ezra looked up from the table where he sat with a bunch of papers, mail, bills, and his laptop sitting in front of him.

"Phoebe. I have a favor to ask of you."

"Oh boy. Don't tell me you're going to ask me to go to jail for you, too, are you?" she asked, exchanging a silly smile with Mina.

"Um, who's going to jail?" Ezra looked confused.

She stood back while Mina explained what was going on.

"No. I don't need you to go to jail for me, not now, and hopefully not ever. That is probably a little bit more than one sibling should ask of another."

"I'm in agreement with that," Phoebe said easily, walking to the refrigerator and taking out some seasoned boiled eggs that she'd made over the weekend for Mina to snack on when she got home from school. She set the container down on the table, and pulled the plastic wrap back. Mina smiled and thanked her before picking up an egg and biting into it.

Ezra picked up an egg, too, but before he bit into it he said, "I've hired someone to help us get the rodeo together this fall. It's just so much more than what we have the expertise for, and I figured we needed someone who knew what they were doing if it was going to have any chance of succeeding."

"I agree. We've been ranchers all our lives, but none of us have done much with the rodeo. We've been too busy working," Phoebe said, picking up an egg for herself. She needed to check supper, which was in the crockpot, and go down the list of groceries that she was going to need in order to make the meals she had planned for this weekend when their visitors to the dude ranch were around. She might have to make a trip into town to get groceries.

"I was hoping you would help me with that."

"Help you?" she asked, surprised. She didn't know anything more than any of her other siblings about the rodeo. Less, possibly.

"Well, I just wanted you to partner with the new guy. He's got all the expertise we need, but I need someone to organize it, pull it all together. He can do the technical things we don't know anything about, but you were the one who always does such a great job of keeping us on track, making a schedule, figuring out the things that we need, and assigning jobs to people. I was hoping that you would work hand-in-hand with him, so that it goes off without a hitch." Ezra paused. "I know you're busy with cooking, and all the other things you do to make the ranch home. I don't want to burden you with more."

It wasn't a burden. She would do anything for her family. She loved to stay busy. She loved to be in the center of everything, and she loved to think what she was doing made a difference.

"It's not a burden. I'm happy to do it."

"Well, he's going to be here in a few weeks, and I'm hoping that you can be his working partner. Obviously, you don't have to spend every waking hour with him, but I told him we would have someone coordinating with him, and when I said that, you were the one I had in mind."

"Of course. No problem. I'd love to." And it was true. She enjoyed organizing things, and she didn't think Ezra would hire anyone who wasn't upright and a man of character.

"He's been divorced, and it wasn't an amicable one. He lost his ranch, and he said he was too old to start over. But, the guy knows what he's doing, so I think he'll be a good addition around here. I was thinking, depending on how things go, and whether we can afford it or not, that I would keep him around indefinitely, because he has all of the experience we lack, particularly when it comes to the sports side of ranching, which can be another area where we can make money to keep the ranch afloat."

"All right. That sounds good to me. I'll do my best to make sure that everything is a success, and that you don't have to worry about whether or not we can pay him. He definitely sounds like he'll be an asset to the ranch." He also sounded like an older fellow who would be retiring any day. So maybe he wouldn't be around forever. Or maybe he'd end up being like a grandfather to Mina, and all of her nieces and nephews who would hopefully be growing up on the ranch.

He could never take her father's place, of course, but he could still be a type of grandfather. Maybe she was getting ahead of herself. She hadn't even met him, and already she was giving him the title of grandfather.

Alice and Hugo, Ezra's and Alaska's children ran into the kitchen, chasing each other, running to Ezra's chair and stopping on either side of him. Ezra pushed back far enough to pick them up and set one on each knee as they squealed and chattered.

The kids were pretty rambunctious and it didn't surprise Phoebe at all when Ezra started to sing. That's the way her parents had always calmed the twelve of them down, too. Or made jobs easier, like picking peas or shelling beans. They'd sung while doing everything growing up.

She recognized the song and joined Ezra in harmony as naturally as breathing, continuing to work with Alaska, smiling as they sang.

I once walked Earth's lonesome road, with a great and heavy load,
Burdened by the shackles of my sin.
'Til I heard the Savior say, I will take your sins away,
Repent, my friend, and turn your face toward Him.
I'll break the chains that bind,

I'll loose the scales that blind,
I'll give you life, I'll give you joy, I'll ease your mind.
And then when your life is o'er, I'll call you home to Heaven's shore.
Come unto me I'll break the chains that bind.
I didn't not come on that day I'd rather live my life my way,
So further down in darkness did I fall.
No longer could I cope, and I lost all trace of hope
But once again I heard the Savior call:
I'll break the chains that bind,
I'll loose the scales that blind,
I'll give you life, I'll give you joy, I'll ease your mind.
And then when your life is o'er, I'll call you home to Heaven's shore.
Come unto me I'll break the chains that bind.
I finally bowed down on my knees, crying "Save my soul, Lord please."
And Jesus heard my painful, desperate sound.
His blood cleansed my soul pure white,
I'm now guiltless in His sight.
Glory to His name I'm Heaven bound.
I'll break the chains that bind,
I'll loose the scales that blind,
I'll give you life, I'll give you joy, I'll ease your mind.
And then when your life is o'er, I'll call you home to Heaven's shore.
Come unto me I'll break the chains that bind.

The kids had calmed and Phoebe listened to the chatter in the kitchen, moving around, checking the crockpot, looking at the items in the pantry and getting her list on her phone. Thinking about how much she loved her family, and how grateful she was that God had allowed her to live the life that she had. She didn't want any regrets, and if she occasionally longed to have a life partner of her own, she would push that aside, and continue to walk the path that the Lord laid out for her, with gratitude, if only for the fact that she was no longer under the bondage of sin. Ezra's song had been a perfect reminder. Almost like he'd done it on purpose, but she knew better. It had been God.

Chapter Twenty-Eight

Lucas stood in front of the apartment door at the back of the library, straightening his shirt, and running a hand over his carefully combed hair, before raising his hand to knock.

It had been two weeks since he and Ryland had stood at the courthouse in Rockerton and said vows to each other.

She had been out to the farm every evening since she said she would do the goats. Despite the stitches in her leg, that had recently been removed, and despite the fact that she had had an auspicious beginning. He hadn't been kidding when he had said trial by fire, but she took it with grace and humor and made him love her even more.

Anyone who could handle blood and an emergency room visit with as much aplomb as she had, was a woman who was worth any effort he needed in order to win her.

They'd been practicing kissing, and the thought made him smile.

Tonight they were going out on a date. And, he had a feeling it was going to be a good bit different than the first date that they had been on, where he had struggled to find anything to say.

Since the dam broke, such as it was, they hadn't had a problem figuring out what to say to each other. In fact, he wasn't sure which he enjoyed more, talking to her or kissing her.

He laughed. He knew exactly which one he enjoyed the most.

He rapped on the door, and it wasn't five seconds later that it opened, as though Ryland had been standing on the other side waiting.

Maybe she had.

"You're right on time!" she said, not giving him a chance to walk in, but stepping out and wrapping her arms around him, lifting her face for his kiss.

He loved it that he got to see a side of her that no one else saw. She did seem to be relaxed and happy on the farm, but she was still the same quiet librarian in the library.

"I would have been early, but I figured that you wanted me to at least not smell like cow manure on our first married date."

"I don't really care how you smell, although," she sniffed the air, "you do smell very good."

"Thank you. I take it the shower washed all the smell off." They had been working cattle that morning, and he'd gotten pretty messy.

"You want to come in and see Grace?"

"Sure do." She backed away, grabbing his hand, and tugging gently. Not that she needed to, he would follow her anywhere, and he did, closing the door behind them.

They went back together, and she said, "I can't believe how much the puppies have grown. Their eyes are open, and they have such sweet little personalities. You can definitely tell a difference in them."

"That's exciting. Another couple weeks and they'll be big enough for us to move them out to the farm if you want. I actually have two people who are interested in one. I had pictures on my phone and I just happened to be chatting with one of the dude ranch visitors yesterday afternoon. I couldn't explain exactly what kind of dogs they were, and admitted that I had no clue who the father was, but they seem to want one anyway."

"I want them to go to good homes. People who won't decide that they made a rash decision, and give them away."

"Of course. That's what we always want. But, sometimes things just don't turn out the way we think they're going to, and we have to adjust. Sometimes people, sometimes animals suffer."

She didn't say anything, and he thought about Mina, how she'd suffered because her parents had decided they no longer wanted to be together. It was probably about the same when someone adopted an animal, and decided it was too much for them. Of course, a person didn't make vows when they adopted an animal, but it was pretty much the same thing. They just decided that wasn't going to work out. The difference being, with a marriage, when they made vows, they were before God.

But it wasn't for him to judge. He hadn't walked in anyone else's shoes, and he couldn't say what he would do if he were faced with a situation like his sister Priscilla had been in. Perhaps divorce was the best thing for her children, but the problem was, her ex had ended up spending just as much time, if not more, with them.

Sometimes life just wasn't fair.

They knelt by the box that he had made. It took up most of the mudroom, but it gave Grace and her puppies plenty of room to move around.

"We'll definitely want to get them out to the ranch once they start moving a little bit more. There's not enough room here."

"I have no idea what I would do without you. I wouldn't want to be keeping these puppies for eight weeks in the mudroom. That's not fair to them, not to mention it would smell terrible."

"Patrons would complain that the library stinks."

"That they would," she said cheerfully, like it didn't matter to her, although he knew she tried to make a trip to the library as pleasant of an experience as possible. Some people went there just to have some quiet time, and Ryland was very aware of that. She was a great librarian. He almost felt a little bit selfish for the question that he planned to ask her tonight. He...wanted to move in with her, living at the library, until they could afford to build a house on the farm.

He wasn't sold on that, and if that's not what Ryland wanted, he would be okay with it. Still, he really wanted to wake up and look out his window at the ground they worked, and the animals they cared for. More importantly, he wanted to wake up beside Ryland. So he supposed wherever she wanted to be, that's where he would be too. If that was okay with her.

They got ready, making sure Grace had plenty of water before they left.

"You still up for going to Rockerton?" he asked as he opened the door for her and she got in his truck.

"I am, if you are."

"I'm happy wherever we go, as long as you're with me."

"That's a great answer. It makes me feel bad. I should've said that."

He laughed, and closed the door, walking around the truck, smiling and wanting to whistle. He hadn't realized that being with someone could make him so happy, with an all day long happiness that never seemed to fade. He supposed they were in the honeymoon stage of their relationship, and they were sure to be tested with whatever trials God planned to put them through, although their first emergency room visit had gone fairly well.

They chatted about the weather, about the work he'd done on the farm that day with the cows, and Ryland said she hoped she could be there when they worked the cattle again. He did too. Maybe that was a good opening to tell her he wanted to move in with her, but it felt like it was too early in the evening, so they chatted more, and the trip to Rockerton flew by.

Once they were seated at the restaurant, he said, "Already this date is so much different than our others."

"Because we're actually talking to each other?"

"Yes. And I have zero plans to eat your food, so there's that, too."

"That's a little disappointing, because I was going to order something I was sure you'd like."

She blinked innocent eyes at him over her menu and he laughed outright, making the couple at the table beside them glance over.

He grinned at them, just because he was so happy he could hardly stand it. He held his menu in one hand, reaching across the table and taking Ryland's hand in his. She smiled at the contact and threaded her fingers through his. Yeah, this date was so much better than any of their others.

"Thank you for sticking with me, even though dating me was a nightmare at first," she said, some of the glow fading from her face.

"How can you say that? You were being exactly who you are! I was the one who is supposed to be able to talk to anyone and was too intimidated to get it together for you. I'm the one who should be thanking you."

"So we're going to argue about it?"

"No. You're going to admit I'm right." Rather than giving her time to argue, he continued. "How about I change the subject - I love you."

Her eyes widened, then narrowed. "That is not fair!"

"All's fair in love and war. And I do. I love you and I want you to know it."

"You did not win that argument, but we can pause it, because I have to say, I love you, too. Truly. And for a long time. Probably about the time you checked out Toenail Fungus - a History in Pictures."

"Ouch. Did I really check that out?"

"You did. And you didn't even read it!!"

"That's because I was besotted with the librarian - I loved her - and I just needed an excuse to be in the library."

"That was some excuse." She grinned.

The waitress came then and took their orders. Lucas had to smile when Ryland ordered something he knew he wasn't going to be the slightest bit tempted to eat - some kind of beet salad with goat cheese.

After the waitress left, he moved his thumb over her hand and said, "Are you really going to eat that? Or did you just order it to make me laugh - or to keep me from being tempted to take your food?"

Her smile flipped his heart. "I ordered it because I have every intention of eating today, unlike our other dates. I don't know why my appetite was totally missing when we ate before, but I'd guess it was for the same reason you couldn't talk."

They shared a look with compassion and awareness flowing between them.

"We've come a long way."

"I agree. But I think we have even farther to go. Well, there really isn't an ultimate destination, is there?" Her brows pinched together.

"This is one of those, enjoy the journey type of thing. And I honestly can't think of anyone I'd rather take this journey with than you."

"And I have my perfect traveling companion, too." Her eyes glowed.

This was the exact wrong time. They could be interrupted by the waitress at any second and the couple beside them were close enough to hear them if they tried, most likely, but Lucas found the words tumbling out of his mouth.

"So, since I built those shelves, the library is pretty full."

"It is. That makes me sad, because it means that in order to purchase more books, I'll have to part with some of the books I have. And, while I think I could pretty much look at your check out history to get a good idea of books no one would ever read, the idea of getting rid of any books makes me sad."

"What if you used your apartment, took the walls down, put some shelves up and turned it into a part of the library?"

Her brows raised.

He held his breath. Waiting. Hoping. Praying.

"That's a great idea," she said slowly. "But there's this small problem of where I would live..." There was a hopeful note in her voice that gave him courage he didn't realize he possessed.

"What if you...lived on the ranch with me?"

Time seemed to slow to a crawl as expressions flickered over her face. Disbelief. Excitement. Hope. Love?

"Yes."

He laughed. "That's it?"

"Yes. Where you are is where I want to be. What is that verse? Where you go, I will go. Where you stay, I will stay. Your God will be my God and your people, my people."

"From Ruth."

"Yes."

"She was talking to Naomi, her mother-in-law."

"But the idea is there, and it applies to me. I go with you. Wherever that is. As long as you want me, and maybe even if you don't. You might not be able to get rid of me."

"No wonder you didn't want to sign that contract."

"Right. It's not about what you're going to do for me. For me, it's about what I'm going to do for you. I'm not concerned with what you're doing."

"That's how I feel - it's about what I can do for you." He paused. "If more people had that attitude, there wouldn't be so much divorce."

"No. That's not a word I ever want to say. You can throw it out. It doesn't apply here."

"I like the way she thinks."

The waitress came and set their meals down in front of them. A rare steak with a baked potato for him and her beet and goat cheese salad. They were opposites in more ways than one. And he realized she really had ordered food just for him, knowing what he wanted and what he liked. It warmed him the whole way to his soul to know that she'd paid attention to him, his likes and dislikes, even when they weren't speaking.

"So, where on the farm were you thinking we'd live?" Ryland asked, a forkful of greens held in the air.

"There really isn't a place for us right now, unless we used my bedroom in the big farmhouse." He drew in a breath, not wanting to say what he was going to. He wanted to give her the world, not tell her how poor he was. "I don't have the money right now to build anything, either. I...I was hoping I could move in with you. Then, when things turn around, we'll build a place on the ranch somewhere. As fancy as you want." He said that, and hoped that he'd be able to afford it when the time came.

He needn't have worried.

"I don't want anything fancy. Just something simple. I was completely content with the library apartment. Although," she paused and if he wasn't mistaken, her cheeks grew pink. "If we're going to have children, we might need more than one bedroom."

"I'd like kids." He spoke casually, but earnestly. He really did want children. Maybe not twelve. And he noticed she hadn't told him he could move into the library apartment with her.

"Twelve?" she asked, not looking as horrified as he would have thought she would. Twelve kids was a lot, even if he did think it was the best way to grow up - in a big, loving family, loud, crazy, plenty of siblings and love and laughter. A big, solid foundation that made a person feel safe and secure no matter where they were in the world.

"As many as you want. I plan on being beside you no matter what, and we'll take care of our kids together, but I don't want to insist on something that is going to make you miserable."

"Maybe we should just submit to God and allow Him to plan our family?"

His jaw dropped. "That's pretty radical."

"I know. But...isn't that faith? Isn't that the trust that we claim to have? How can we say we're seeking God's plan for our lives, if we don't trust Him with our family size?"

That was a great question and one that he wasn't sure he was ready to answer. He wanted to think he had faith. That he trusted God, but Ryland had just challenged him in a way he hadn't even considered.

"We don't have to make a decision tonight, do we?" he asked.

"No." She took a breath. "But...when you asked if you could move in. When, exactly, were you thinking?"

He swallowed, knife in one hand, a piece of steak in the other. Honesty was the only thing he could pull out of his brain. "Tonight."

"Oh."

He couldn't read her expression beyond the surprise.

"Is that okay?" He found himself praying again.

"Yes. I...I would like that." She gave a tremulous smile that charged every nerve ending in his body. Suddenly he was the one who wasn't the slightest bit hungry.

"I...I'm not going to eat any more of my salad," she murmured softly.

"I don't want to seem like I want to starve you to death, but I'm ready to go, too."

"Let's."

They stood, his eyes scanning the room for their waitress. He found her, paid the bill and, grabbing his wife's hand, they left the restaurant. It was definitely not the slightest bit like any of their other dates, and not only because once they made it back to Sweet Water, he didn't drive home.

Epilogue

Alaska moved her foot along Ezra's bare leg, stretching like a cat after a good afternoon nap. Maybe she felt a little like said cat. Ezra had a way of making her feel happy clear down to her bones.

"Ezra?" she said softly, her hand on her stomach where the baby she'd told him about earlier in the evening nestled.

"Hmm?" he said, obviously almost asleep.

She almost said "nevermind" because he really did have a lot on his shoulders. He took his position as eldest of twelve and unofficial head of the Sweet View Ranch very seriously.

But...she was worried and she knew he could calm her fears.

"Do you think it was a good idea to hire Tillman and to put Phoebe and him in such close contact?"

Ezra had come awake at her words. She could feel the change in his body. She snuggled closer, molding her limbs to his.

"I don't think it's going to hurt anything, and it could possibly work out the way we hope it will."

"You don't think they'll hate each other?"

"Phoebe gets along with everyone. Tillman might be a little bitter after his divorce, but again, I think Phoebe will be perfect for him. He's a good man."

Ezra had gone to college with Tillman back in the day. They'd been roommates and best friends. They'd stayed in touch, with each of them working their own ranch, they'd often called each other for advice or to ask questions only another rancher would know the answer to. Ranching wasn't like most professions, say, teaching, where co-workers could meet in the faculty lounge and chat.

"I'm just worried. I don't want anything to happen to Phoebe. I've...I've come to love her like a sister, and I know she's such a sweetheart. She'd do anything for anyone and maybe Tillman is too bitter and jaded for him to realize what a treasure she is. Or to treat her the way she deserves to be treated."

Ezra was quiet for a bit. She knew he was thinking. Another man might have gone back to sleep, but Ezra would take her concerns seriously, even if she waited to voice them until after midnight and just as he was falling asleep. That's just the kind of man he was. Sometimes she had to pinch herself to believe that she was actually married to such an honorable and compassionate man.

"I don't want to be trite, but you know the saying, 'Nothing ventured, nothing gained?' Sometimes we have to put ourselves out there, take a risk, step out by faith, before we get the good things God has for us. Now, I know, Phoebe isn't stepping out by faith, that's mostly you and me. Both of us are going to be hurt if Phoebe gets hurt, but she's been so devoted to her family, I think you're right that she needed a little push."

"I hope so. I guess I was just getting cold feet and I needed you to tell me everything was going to be okay."

"I can't make that promise, but I can say that Tillman is a good man. Bitter, and maybe a little sour on women, but still a man of character. He is not going to hurt my sister on purpose."

That was what she needed to hear. Again. Since Ezra had already told her that. Several times, in fact. But for some reason, hearing it over again, helped ground her and settled her fears.

"He needs a woman who is above reproach. Someone who doesn't have a hint of guile in her. Who has a spotless reputation. Phoebe more than fits the bill."

"You're right. That's what I needed to hear." She ran a hand up his stomach and over his chest. "Thank you for taking the time to reassure me."

"Always. I always have time for you."

"Maybe I can make that lost sleep worth your while," she whispered, her hand moving down his chest, then lower.

"Hmm." Ezra's lips moved across her temple. "I'm listening."

"Good. Let me tell you what I have in mind." She smiled in the dark as she moved against him and his hands came around her, sliding down her back.

Ezra was right. There was nothing to worry about. And she had her own marriage, her own amazing, God-sent man, to care for.

She pushed thoughts of Phoebe and Tillman aside and focused on enjoying her own husband.

~

Join Jessie's list and be the first to know about new releases and sales on her books!

Read *A Cowboy's Calm Strength*, the next story from Sweet View Ranch in which Phoebe Clyborne makes the worst kind of first impression on her new ranch foreman. When Tillman gets assigned to work with the drunken criminal to organize a rodeo, he'll have to learn that appearances can be deceiving in order to see God is giving him a second chance of his own.

*Sneak Peek of A Cowboy's
Calm Strength*

Phoebe tapped her finger on the metal bar. She had been curious about a lot of things in her life, but one of the things she had never wondered about was what life looked like from behind the vertical, cold steel bars of prison.

She had found out anyway.

"Rich, how much longer?"

"You know you're like a two-year-old on a car trip, right?" Rich said from where he sat behind the big corner desk, his feet propped up on the one spot that wasn't covered with papers, old take-out wrappers, and bottles of pain pills. He held a steaming cup of coffee in one hand with his other hand hooked on his belt loop, his fingers resting lightly over the radio clip there.

"I'm sorry. If you hadn't taken my watch, I wouldn't need to ask." Phoebe felt like a petulant child. She understood that the lock-in was supposed to simulate real life. When she agreed to do it for the Sweet Water High fundraiser, she figured it wasn't going to be a walk in the park, and neither did she expect that.

Originally it was supposed to be on a Friday night, but the jail had been too crowded, so it had been moved to a weekday. She appreciated that. But it was almost time for her to be let out, and she didn't want to stay one second longer than what she had to. She'd signed up for twelve hours, found ten people to pledge ten dollars an hour, and had raised twelve hundred dollars for the high school. But twelve hours was it.

Rich was not the kind of guy who was going to be early or even super concerned about letting her out on time. It was up to her.

"We don't allow regular prisoners to keep their watches, so why would we let you keep yours? This is supposed to be the real deal."

"I know. I won't ask again, if you'll just let me know how much longer." She made that promise, hoping she could keep it. Surely it had been at least an hour since she'd asked the last time, and at that point, she'd had one hour and twenty-seven minutes left.

"You promise?" Rich said with a brow raised.

"I do."

"And if you break your promise, what do I get?"

She almost huffed out a breath. She was thirty-six years old and not exactly the kind of person who inspired romantic interest in men. She'd figured that out a long time ago, back in her twenties when she was raising her siblings and no one was interested in her.

She'd given up the idea that she would ever get married. And maybe, after what her twin had gone through with her marriage, it had been a good decision. Although she would have liked to have had a husband and children. She wanted that. But it seemed like God had her serving her own family, her brothers and sisters, and stepping in after her parents had died. She mostly accepted that and didn't long for a family of her own.

Much, anyway.

"What do you want?" she asked with resignation.

"You ask me again, and you're gonna watch my kids next Friday night while I go on a date."

"Done," she said easily. Yeah, she didn't think he was actually going to want her to do anything with him. Just watch his kids.

So, one night in the lockup hadn't changed anything in that regard.

She waited while he pulled his phone out of his front shirt pocket and tilted it so it kicked on, trying not to be impatient.

He said the time, and she calculated in her head that she had twenty-three minutes left.

Monday night had been a good choice, since there hadn't been any other...prisoners? Patrons? What was it called when a person was put in jail?

Anyway, she had been alone all night, which had been just fine with her, although she wouldn't have minded keeping her phone at the very least. She could read a book or something. As it was, she'd occupied herself by staring at the cell wall while trying not to think about how dirty the mattress was behind her. Or how many other people had slept on it.

It wasn't that the jail was filthy, because it wasn't. Not really. Not compared to their barn on the ranch. But she figured out that she was a little claustrophobic and more of a germaphobe than she wanted to admit. At least when it came to prison cells. Who knew?

Sighing, she turned away from the bars, walked back over, and sat down on the mat where she'd spent most of the last twelve hours. Drawing her feet up, she leaned back against the wall. She hadn't slept very well, and she was tired, but she had a full morning's worth of work to do when she got released.

Her family had been working hard to make their dude ranch a success, and they'd decided to host a rodeo this year. It would draw people in, let people know about the ranch, and hopefully get them some bookings for next spring and summer. If not this fall. Cold came to North Dakota early, but fall was still a beautiful time of year here.

Winter was pretty too, and they were thinking about getting some draft horses and doing sleigh rides at least through the holiday season.

But Phoebe had been put in charge of the rodeo.

Her, along with a new guy that they had hired just for that...to coordinate the rodeo and help them run it. They were planning on keeping him on as a full-time employee afterward, if things went well.

Tillman Snyder was the man's name, and he was supposed to show up at the ranch first thing this morning.

Phoebe didn't know much else about him other than he had been her brother's college roommate and her brother, Ezra, had asked her to work with him to get things organized. She was known as being particular and meticulous in recordkeeping, plus she would organize the food and games and prizes as well as the decorations and the arrangements on the ranch, while he took care of all of the things that she didn't really know much about—the events themselves, getting the temporary corrals and everything else set up, and she didn't even know what all else.

But hopefully, Tillman and she would be able to combine their strengths and make the rodeo a smashing success. To say that the future of their ranch depended on it wasn't an overexaggeration.

She tapped her hand on her leg, figuring that twenty-three minutes had gone by long ago, but she'd promised she wasn't going to ask again.

Stealing a glance underneath her lashes at Rich, she wondered if he was deliberately not telling her her time was up so that she would ask again, so he'd have a free babysitter Friday night. She wouldn't put it past him.

Finally, she got up, and while she wasn't much of a pacer, she walked over to the end of the jail cell and back. She hadn't realized that she was claustrophobic. Last night had told her that much. That was probably the reason she wanted out more than anything. She had been trying to keep her mind occupied, thinking about other things, paramount among those the rodeo, but now that she knew her time was surely up, the walls felt like they were closing in, and it drove her crazy that she couldn't escape.

Not to mention, she had to use the bathroom, and she was absolutely not using the urinal that the cell provided.

She supposed she could probably complain. Surely there were discrimination laws that stated that a female prisoner needed to have facilities that suited her physiology. And privacy as well.

But considering that it was only twelve hours and that her time was up, she would be happy if Rich would simply let her out.

She went over and stood as close to him as she could get, trying to remind him that she was there, and it was time for her to leave.

He pretended not to notice.

She knew he was pretending, because she saw his eyes glance up and his lips quirk a little, and then he looked back down at the iPad that was balanced above his knees after taking a sip of his coffee.

Smelling the coffee made her stomach rumble and her mouth water.

She usually started the day with at least two cups, but no one had offered her coffee. Or food of any kind.

Not that she had expected anything. After all, the jail was allowing them to do this as a matter of public service and kindness; she didn't want to cost the county any extra money.

She drew a breath in through her nose and blew it out her mouth. She was not going to say anything. And then she thought, why not? Did it really matter if she went to wherever Rich lived and watched his kids for an evening? It wasn't like she was typically super busy on Friday night. But she wasn't going to if she didn't have to.

"Rich?"

His head drew up slowly, and there was a small smirk, arrogant and irritating, that turned up the corner of one of his lips. "Are you asking me what time it is? Because, you do remember our deal, correct?"

"Correct. I remember. And you're right. I'm not asking, but if you happen to check…"

He gave her a look, knowing that now that she'd mentioned it, he could hardly continue to keep her past her time. With a put-out sigh, he uncrossed his legs and dropped them to the floor, grabbing the large key that worked the lock. She had expected everything to be electronic. Although, she hadn't really thought about whether or not the jail in Rockerton, North Dakota, would have entered the twenty-first century. If she had thought about it, she would have expected there to be some kind of electronic locks. But there wasn't.

"Aren't you going to look at your phone?" she asked.

"Don't need to. The timer on the desk that they set when the kids locked you in here last night went off twenty minutes ago."

"I didn't hear it."

"That's because I shut it off before it could go off."

"You did it on purpose?"

"Yeah?" he said, not bothering to try to hide his smirk. "You have no idea how expensive babysitters are nowadays."

She wanted to say something about the word sucker being stamped on her forehead and she didn't know it, but she didn't. She also tried to push away the thought that when a man looked at her, he saw sucker and babysitter, not siren and kissable, or any other romantic words, which showed how pathetic she was. She didn't even know any romantic words that she could use to describe herself.

Instead, she waited while he opened her cell door, then kept her irritation in check when he asked for her phone number—in case he needed a babysitter, a paid one—and programmed it into his phone.

"I'll give you a call at some point to see if you can watch the kiddos for me."

She nodded, then as she was sticking her phone back in her pocket, she said, "I could be a serial killer, you know."

He laughed. "I watched you for the last twelve hours. I definitely trust my kids with you. You're harmless and more than a little boring." He grinned. "No offense. That's actually a compliment, since I'm thinking about hiring you to watch my children."

She nodded, not liking the way her life had turned out, exactly, but laughing to herself that he had pinned her so correctly. She was serious, responsible, and, yeah, boring.

But at least she had made twelve hundred dollars for the Sweet Water high school. Even if she did end up with a babysitting gig she really didn't want because of it.

She shook her head. She wasn't going to have time to babysit, not if they were going to get the rodeo planned now and set up in two short months. She could always say no when he called.

She had to admit, as she stepped out of the jailhouse and started down the steps, that it felt great to be outside. Hopefully the little bit of claustrophobia she felt while locked up was not something that was going to erupt into a full-blown issue.

Maybe she'd been cooped up for too long, or maybe she was hungrier than she thought, because as she stepped down the steps, lifting her eyes to the sky and taking a deep breath of the warm late spring air, she lost her balance and started tumbling down the steps.

Sign up for Jessie's newsletter! Get a free book, access to exclusive bonus content, get fun and funny updates on her life on the farm and more!

A Gift from Jessie

View this code through your smart phone camera to be taken to a page where you can download a FREE ebook when you sign up to get updates from Jessie Gussman! Find out why people say, "Jessie's is the only newsletter I open and read" and "You make my day brighter. Love, love, love reading your newsletters. I don't know where you find time to write books. You are so busy living life. A true blessing." and "I know from now on that I can't be drinking my morning coffee while reading your newsletter – I laughed so hard I sprayed it out all over the table!"

Claim your free book from Jessie!